Keep Your Songs

In Your Heart

A Story of Friendship and Hope

during World War II

by Carolyn Summer Quinn

Dedication

My parents grew up during World War II and raised me on stories of what their life was once like on the "American home front." One of our finest moments as a family came when I asked them to read through my first draft of **KEEP YOUR SONGS IN YOUR HEART** to make sure I'd written all the little details of the time period correctly. We had such fun discussing it.

My father absolutely loved this story of the gutsy and loyal little girl named Ruby and couldn't wait to see it in print. So, Patrick Francis Henry Quinn (1928-2018) – "Frank" to his friends and "Daddy" to me - this one's **for YOU!**

Chapter One: Aiming for the Stars

Seattle, December 6, 1941

It was the Saturday before the Sunday that changed everything, but my best friend

Emiko Fujiwara and I didn't know it yet.

"Shine little glow-worm, glimmer, glimmer,

Shine little glow-worm, glimmer glimmer!"

We were walking along our block on First Avenue North in Seattle, heading for the

movie theater, inhaling the clear December air, tinged with the scent of pine trees. We

were also rehearsing the songs we would perform later that month at the Sixth Grade

Talent Show - at the top of our lungs. The show was set to happen right before

Christmas vacation.

"Lead us lest too far we wander," Emi, as everyone called her, sang her solo part as we

walked in step with one another.

"Love's sweet voice is calling yonder!" I belted mine, not realizing that this particular

bright Saturday was one I would always remember, later, as the last day of normalcy.

That afternoon we had no idea what was coming, and neither did President Franklin

Delano Roosevelt, not to mention the United States Army and Navy. It wasn't love's sweet voice.

The date was December 6, 1941.

Within twenty-four hours there would be trouble. Lots of it. We continued on together:

"Shine little glow-worm, glimmer, glimmer,
Shine little glow-worm, glimmer, glimmer,
Light the path below, above,
And lead us on to love!"

Love was actually the last thing that was on the way. We passed by a house where a man busy working on his car in the driveway, a spanking new Pontiac, growled, "Pipe down, you two, will ya? I can't hear myself think to fix this radiator with you girls making such a racket. You're disturbing the peace!"

"Hooray!" Emi replied merrily.

"The peace has been officially disturbed!" I declared. "By us!"

Laughing, we moved along and went right on singing as loud as we could. That man didn't realize it, but piping down was not in either one of our natures. My father always said that Emi and I were born boisterous. He was right, though it was Emi who was the real expert at it. She didn't go down steps one at a time if it was faster to jump the last three. She sometimes cartwheeled across the lawn from her house to mine instead of just walking. I even remembered how, when we were about four, she wouldn't get into her father's car through the door if he left it parked with the window open. She'd let out a war whoop worthy of Tarzan, approach the car at a run, take a jump, and then dash in through the window.

After she did that a few times and wound up needing stitches for cutting her head somehow, her father had to make sure he always shut the car window, and it wasn't because of the Seattle tendency for rain. It was to keep Emi from breaking her neck.

That song was the first of two we were singing in the talent show so we continued on, swinging into the other, even louder:

"Be my little baby bumble bee
buzz around, buzz around, keep a-buzzin' 'round
We'll be just as happy as can be
You and me, you and me, you and me..."

Then we got to the best part, the big finish:

"Honey, keep a-buzzin' please
I've got a dozen cousin bees
But I want you to be
My baby bumble bee!"

Mrs. Manning around the corner was out in her front yard, as usual, raking the leaves dropped by her maple tree. She cheered us on, "You sound great, girls!" The day was cold, and damp in the piercing way late autumn days in the Pacific Northwest could be, where a chill seemed to enter straight into your bones, stay there, and not get back out again. We were wearing woolen skirts with matching cardigan sweaters, mine red, Emi's royal blue, over heavy blouses under winter coats, but still, it was raw and damp. We skipped down the street. It helped keep us a wee bit warmer.

But even if the weather had been a lot more pleasant, Emi and I probably would have been scampering along at a fast pace anyway. We liked a lot of activity, and so much the better if we could sing at the same time as we ran.

Those two songs, "Glow Worm" and "Be My Little Baby Bumble Bee," were not our first choice to perform in the talent show. They were very old songs, not the new ones showcased every week on the radio program Emi and I and just about everyone else we knew loved to listen to, *Your Hit Parade*. Emi and I both thought these two numbers were rather babyish for sixth graders like us, but our fabulous teacher, Mrs. Rivington, had asked us to sing them because they were two of her favorites. We liked her too much to say no.

The one we had really wanted to sing was suggested by another teacher, Miss Bryce, who lived on our street, a few houses away from us, which she seemed to think gave her the right to regularly butt into our conversations and business. Miss Bryce looked and talked a bit like Popeye the Sailor Man from the cartoons and had taught us in the fifth grade. She overheard Emi and me wondering in the schoolyard what to sing in the show, so she made her way over to us and said, "May I suggest my all-time favorite? It's called 'A Good Man Is Hard to Find!'" She cackled like a pirate at that and strode away in her long forest green skirt and square black ugly lace-up shoes, never expecting we'd find sheet music for the song at the music store and would actually want to sing it.

We did find it. We loved it! It sounded sophisticated, like something our favorite movie stars, Carole Lombard and Marlene Dietrich, might sing in a movie. The song went:

"A good man is hard to find,

You always get the other kind

Just when you think that he's your pal,

You look for him and find

Him fooling 'round some other gal..."

Mrs. Rivington clutched her double strand of pearls, the way she did when something worried her, when Emi and I sang it for her. She said if she were to let us perform such a number it might get the parents in an uproar, and she didn't want a riot on her hands in the school auditorium. That's when she suggested "Glow Worm" and "Bumble Bee," telling us she and her own best friend used to love to sing them when they were young, which must have been at least thirty long years ago, maybe even forty. "My best friend and I weren't very good singers, I'm afraid," Mrs. Rivington said with a twinkle in her pretty green eyes when she suggested Emi and I sing the two "bug" songs in the class show. "I think you two, who are so much better at carrying a tune, could sing them with a lot more style and pizzazz." Then with her eyes sparkling, Mrs. Rivington had winked

7

and added, "I've also been thinking of a fun new way of introducing you two. Rather than just calling you Ruby Carol Rafferty and Emiko Fujiwara, how do you like the idea of being billed as 'Ruby and Emerald, the Gemstone Girls?'"

Emi and I had squealed at once.

"I love it," Emi smiled.

"Me too," I agreed. "The *Gemstone* Girls! Why in the world didn't we think of using a name like that for ourselves sooner?" Our parents had nicknamed us "Ruby and Emerald" when we were still in diapers, so "The Gemstone Girls" sounded perfect for us.

"I've thought of you two best buddies as my Gemstone Girls since the very first day you walked into my classroom in September," Mrs. Rivington grinned. She was always so kind to us. "It sounds like the name of a show business act. The way you two can sing like a dream, who knows? You know what I always tell my students, don't you?"

We sure did. "Hitch your wagon to a star!" Emi and I chorused in unison. It was her favorite quote, she had told the class on the first day of school. It meant that if you were going to be pulled around in a wagon or chariot anyway, then hitch it to a star, not a horse. Aiming for the stars could get you clear off the ground. The quote hung on the wall of our classroom.

Mrs. Rivington said it was also about having what she called "the best possible attitude." With the right can-do outlook, she said, we could go anywhere and do anything. "Not even the sky is the limit anymore," she loved to tell us, "especially now that the world's got airplanes!"

"That's it exactly! Hitch your wagon to a star," she said to the idea of Emi and I having an act. "Then maybe someday you'll be performing in theaters and nightclubs and appearing on the radio. You'll both be famous! Someday my big claim to fame will be that I once taught you two legends when you were little."

Nightclubs! Theaters! The radio! Emi and me, *legends!* The whole idea of having an act and becoming famous put Emi and me over the moon. We had lived next door to one another our entire lives, and always talked so much about wanting to grow up to be performers, maybe even movie stars, that our parents, who were also friends, had given us a great big surprise just two weeks earlier.

We found out about it on the Sunday right after Thanksgiving. My mother and father told me to put my coat and hat on. Mom put her own hat on top of her upswept auburn hairdo and said we were going to "go somewhere" so they could "announce something" that was "all about Christmas," but they wouldn't tell me anything more than that. "As Santa would say, ho ho ho," Mom told me mysteriously, winking one of her pretty blue eyes.

"It's about Christmas? What is it? Can't you be more specific?" I asked as I got into my coat, left behind the hat I didn't like, and followed them out to our car, a black De Soto, in the driveway.

"We could, I suppose," my father grinned. He was a pleasant-looking man, a newspaper reporter with sandy-colored hair he wore in a crew cut and wire-rimmed glasses over his dark green eyes. I had Dad's hair color and green eyes, both.

"Yes, we sure could. But we don't want to be," teased my mother.

"Come on! *Tell* me," I urged them.

"Should we?" Dad asked Mom with a big grin.

"Oh no! No, no, no! Not yet," my mother answered with a smile. "Not for a little while longer. It's much more fun building the suspense for this kid. You'll find out soon enough, Ruby."

"You'll just have to wait and see what happens next," said Dad.

"At least tell me how long it will take to ride wherever it is that we're going," I tried, hoping the answer to that one would give me a little more information so I could figure out this surprise.

"Five minutes. Ten, tops," said Dad.

I sat bouncing on the back seat, unable to contain my excitement. Seattle was a town that had been built on seven hills. Our house was in a neighborhood just south of Queen Anne Hill, the one with the most scrumptiously royal name of them all. The shopping district was the only place in town I could think of that was ten minutes away, and that might just be our destination. Unfortunately if that was where we were heading, there were so many stores that it didn't help me narrow down the possibilities of which one would hold this Christmas present. Were we going to Nordstrom's or Frederick & Nelson's department stores, or better yet, to my favorite, the Bon Marché? Or maybe might we be headed to one of the other, smaller downtown shops? Did my parents want me to show them what kind of presents I was hoping for? I was getting to be too old for dolls but still liked looking at Emi's porcelain doll collection, beautifully made dolls dressed in long silk gowns called kimonos. They came from her grandmother in Japan. I had always wanted one, though those were too delicate to play with. They were more for decoration purposes and sat on pieces of gray-blue silk that lined a special "doll shelf" made of wood from a fir tree that her father had put up in her bedroom. Besides, these days, at the age of eleven, I was less interested in toys than I used to be, but wild about the movies. I liked the idea of getting a subscription to movie magazine like *Photoplay* a lot more than I wanted a doll. I also could have used some new art supplies. A nice new dress or two would make great gifts, I thought, too. Warm ones, for winter.

We rode not to the shopping district at all but to a neighborhood known as Nihonmachi. It was Seattle's Japantown. There were lots of Japanese shops, including one I loved called the Higo Ten Cent Store that carried items directly from Japan. At the Higo it was possible to find silk fans, parasols, Japanese paintings, including one I had on the wall of my bedroom of a garden in the city of Kyoto, and even toys and dolls. Maybe we were going there for me to select one of those.

Japantown was also where Emi's father had his ice cream parlor. I was surprised when my father parked the car near Mr. Fujiwara's shop.

My curiosity started reaching a fever pitch. Why were we *here*, of all places, and what did the ice cream shop have to do with Christmas?

"Come on," I urged Mom and Dad, "tell me! What's going on?"

"Ah, you're about to find out," Dad drove me crazy even further by answering the question without revealing a thing.

We went inside, the little chimes that hung on the inside of the door ringing to announce our arrival. We found Emi and her mother, along with her new baby sister, Hanae, born in September, already there, waiting for us at a round table. Her father took our orders. We unanimously decided on Coca Colas and hot fudge banana split sundaes.

Mr. Fujiwara gave the order to his helper, his nephew Nicky Kimura. Nicky went up front to make the sundaes and pour the Cokes into the soda glasses, while also taking up the post behind the counter in case any new customers came in. Mr. Fujiwara rarely ever stopped working while he was in the store but sat down at the table, for once, and joined us.

All of the adults could not stop smiling. Even Nicky was smiling. He even seemed like he was ready to burst from having to hold back the secret of why we were there.

Then they told us the good news.

Make that the *great* news.

"We know you girls love movies," Mrs. Fujiwara began.

"We realize movies are your favorite things in the world," said my mother.

"So we've arranged a special surprise for you this year," Dad took up the tale. "Both of you."

Mr. Fujiwara tapped his hands on the table, teasing us with the line, "Drumroll, please!"

"Emi and Ruby," Mom announced, "you're going to be spending this Christmas vacation in Hollywood!"

Hollywood?

Hollywood!

For a moment I didn't - *couldn't* - say anything. Neither could Emi. We exchanged an astonished glance. Could this be real? It was the city we had dreamed about, and hoped to see, for as long as either one of us could remember. It was the home of all of our heroes, the movie stars.

I found my voice first. "Did you really just say 'Hollywood?'" I finally asked the four adults, looking at them to see if any of them were pulling our legs.

They all burst out in great big smiles. "Yes, we sure did!" laughed Mrs. Fujiwara.

Hollywood! It was astonishing to hear we were actually going to get to go there, to see it.

Mom asked me if I remembered her old friend Joy Vandermeer who used to live near us in Seattle. "She's the one who got married several years ago and moved to Los Angeles. Remember? You were at the wedding."

I recalled it vaguely. It had been a summertime wedding, and her bridesmaids had all worn light pink tulle dresses.

"Well," Mom explained, "Joy and her husband moved there and have always wanted us to visit. Their house just happens to be near one of the movie studios. I think you girls will love the location. We're all going to stay with them, Emi, your father, you, and me."

"Hollywood," I said happily, "has always been the town I've wanted to see the most. And now we're going, we're going, *we're going!*" I got up from the table and twirled around in a circle. Mom said to be careful or I'd knock something breakable off the top of our table and some of the others besides.

"I wish I could go also," Mrs. Fujiwara said, "but I can not. Not with our baby only two months old."

"I wish I could go, too," said Emi's father. "Unfortunately I have to stay here and run the ice cream parlor."

"No you don't," said Emi. "Not at Christmas! It's the store's slowest time of the year." Ice cream definitely wasn't as popular in the wintertime as it was in the summer.

"Can't you both take a vacation, too?" I chimed in. "You don't want to miss this!" Emi's parents and mine had become close friends, just like she and I were. We had gone on a vacation to Yosemite National Park two summers ago and all stayed in a big tent my father and Mr. Fujiwara had pitched. This past summer Emi's parents hadn't been able to go with us to the cabin we had rented in the Cascade Mountains because Emi's mother had been expecting Hanae. Emi had gone with us without them.

"Yes, let Cousin Nicky run the place and come with us," Emi urged.

"Oh, Ruby and Emi. What dears you are to want us to join you! I'm sorry, but that just isn't possible at the moment, not with the new baby. You girls go - and have the time of your lives," said Emi's father. "That's an order!" The way he said it, with a wink, we laughed some more. It was so easy to let a laugh bubble up and fly out of my mouth after the news we'd just received. *Hollywood!*

"Oh, I almost forgot," Emi's father added. "I have a present for each of you, too."

"Another present?" Emi asked. "In addition to hearing we're about to get the best one ever?"

Her father went into the back of the shop and came out with a shopping bag. From that he withdrew two boxes, one for each of us. They were wrapped in paper, silver with a red bow on top for me, gold with a green one for Emi.

We tore the paper off. Inside there were brand-new Brownie box cameras. There were also several rolls of extra film. These were wonderful presents!

"You have to promise me," Mr. Fujiwara said, "to take as many Hollywood pictures as possible for your mother and me to see when you get home. That way we'll feel as if we were there, too."

"Are we going to be driving there in the car?" I asked Dad.

"No, we're taking a ride on the train," he replied, "and it's going to be a long trip, but very nice. It involves not one but *two* overnights stays on the choo-choo. You'll get to see something of Portland, Oregon and San Francisco out side of the windows. We'll have bunks in the sleeper car."

"A sleeper car!" Emi squealed.

"This is going to be the best trip of all time! First I want to go to Grauman's Chinese Theater and see the stars' handprints and footprints in the cement. What about you, Emi?"

"The gates of Paramount Pictures Studio."

"Don't stop at the gates. Let's go in!" said my father.

"Then I want to see palm trees," I added.

"And eat at Chasens, like the stars, then go to the beach," said Emi.

"And take a stroll on Sunset Boulevard!" I added. "This is so fantastic! What day do we leave?"

"On Saturday, December 20th," said Dad with a grin. "The day after the talent show. You'll be missing a few days of school the next week, if you wouldn't mind that."

"We won't!" I laughed. "Let's see. There's twenty days in December, and today is November 23rd," I thought out loud. "So there's seven days left in November. That makes twenty-seven more days until we go!"

I almost groaned when I realized how long it would be before we got on the train. Twenty-seven days seemed like an eternity and a half.

"At least it's not twenty-eight," Emi smiled.

"Part of the fun is all in the planning," grinned my mother, "which is why we just had to tell you about it ahead of time."

"We'll be on our way before you know it," Dad said.

"Wow," was all I could say. I found I absolutely couldn't stop smiling. That day, if somebody had offered me a million bucks to wipe the grin off my face for even a moment, there's no way I could have won the money.

Then Nicky came over with banana splits with velvety hot fudge sauce for everybody except baby Hanae and we all dug in.

* * * * *

Now, on the way to the movies thirteen long days of endless waiting but happy planning later, Emi stopped singing just long enough to ask me, "How many days is it until we leave *now?*"

She actually already knew the answer, but asked me anyway, just so we could discuss it and enjoy how much closer we were to our departure than we had been yesterday.

"It's December 6th," I replied happily, "and we leave on the 20th, so…we'll be Hollywood bound in *fourteen days,* and in Hollywood itself in *sixteen!*

"Wow, only two more weeks until we leave!"

We let out a nice, loud squeal as we continued down the street.

Chapter Two: Two New Faces

We went for a detour to Emi's father's shop for ice cream on the way to the movies every Saturday, then stayed at the theater all day long, usually watching the double features twice, and sometimes even three times. We weren't the only ones. Lots of the kids we knew spent their entire Saturdays at the movie theater. We always met most of our class there.

The ice cream parlor was a pretty, airy shop on Sixth Avenue South near South Main Street, located between a Japanese tailor shop and a store that sold books in the Japanese language. The walls were painted peach, and there were little white round tables and chairs with cheerful aqua cushions and coral-colored hearts painted on the chair backs. The minute I walked in there I always felt happy. One of those cute Japanese white ceramic cats with red trim, with one paw raised for luck, sat beside the cash register. I patted it on the head as I went through the door.

Emi's father had just installed a new money-making gimmick in the store: a photo booth. "Try it out, girls," he urged us, giving us a quarter from the cash register. "You can take pictures by yourself or together."

"Let's take them together!" I squealed. "We can pose like we're stars. I'm Carole Lombard!" She was my favorite actress, blonde, stunning and fearless, to the point she once refused pain medicine while needing stitches after an accident. Carole was boisterous, too, like me. LIFE Magazine had said, "When Carole Lombard talks, her conversation, often brilliant, is punctuated by screeches, laughs, growls, gesticulations and the expletives of a sailor's parrot." I hung it up in my room. When Mrs. Rivington had asked everyone in our class to do oral reports on a famous American who inspired us, other kids picked patriotic ones like President Roosevelt, George Washington, Betsy Ross or Amelia Earhart, but I chose Carole Lombard.

Paul Yamaguchi had rolled his eyes and said, "Come on, Ruby, Mrs. Rivington means an *important* American, not a movie star."

I said Carole Lombard was just as important as any of the others because she had the power to make us all laugh, which made people happier. Mrs. Rivington had to stifle a laugh herself at that, but admitted I made a valid point and approved Lombard as my subject.

It was the easiest assignment I ever had to complete since I already knew everything about Carole. She was married to the most handsome actor of all, Clark Gable, nicknamed "The King of Hollywood." They started dating after dancing together at a Hollywood ball. One dance was all it took for a romance to start. They later eloped, so now she was nicknamed Hollywood's Queen.

Best of all, to me, was that my full name was Ruby Carol Rafferty. I didn't spell it with the "e" at the end, like she did, yet I loved it that "Carol" was part of my name, too.

"Well then I'm Marlene Dietrich," Emi declared, mentioning her favorite. Marlene Dietrich was a regal actress who came from Berlin, Germany. She had been Emi's favorite since early last year when she played a saloonkeeper named "Frenchy" in a

Western called *Destry Rides Again.* Emi had gotten in trouble in the fifth grade for singing Marlene's saloon girl number, "See What the Boys in the Back Room will Have and Pour Out the Same Thing for Me," in front of our art teacher. It was sung in the movie in a saloon. The art teacher thought it was such a bad selection that she called Emi's father up at home over it. Emi's father just laughed and started singing the chorus into the receiver. That stopped Mrs. Murray in the middle of her morality lecture. Her plan to get Emi in trouble was fabulously foiled because her dad was too amused to overreact.

Nicky heard Emi's comment about wanting to be Dietrich and called out, "You look more like Anna May Wong, little Emerald-Squirt!"

Anna May Wong was a star from an Asian family, born here in America to Chinese parents. We could have used several more, actually. There were movies where white people wearing makeup played Japanese characters. The most famous one was Sidney Toler, who played the Chinese detective Charlie Chan. He wasn't Chinese. He had Scottish ancestors and came from Missouri.

I always thought that was strange. There were enough Asian people in the United States for the movie studios to hire a few real ones.

"So vhat? Do I care eef I don't look like Marlene Dietrich? I *feel like* Marlene Dietrich," Emi replied, putting on a fake German accent.

"Vell not matter vhat you feel like, you look like a Japanese Empress," Nicky used an accent right back. Those two always had a wonderful time teasing one another, like siblings. It made me wish I had a big handsome cousin nearby, too. Mom told me I had lots of them, but they were all in New York, where she and Dad were originally from.

"Ze less Asian stars zhere are now," I said, also trying to do the German accent, "ze more of a chance zere vill be for Emi to be one later."

"*Vun* later, you mean," said Nicky.

"Yes, *vun*," I agreed. But so much laughter bubbled up inside of me that I couldn't talk straight enough to add anything else.

Into the photo booth Emi and I went, with me tossing my hair and Emi putting one hand on her hip, both of us smiling for all we were worth. Four little photos came out in a strip. We borrowed a scissors from behind the counter to cut it in half. I kept the top two Emi took the ones on the bottom.

Our favorite movie theater was the Fifth Avenue, the biggest and prettiest one in Seattle, designed to resemble a real Chinese palace with lots of red and gold gilt on the lavish interior and even royal blue murals of dragons decorating the walls. It was almost a three-mile hike from our block to get there, but we gladly made the weekly expedition, going up and down the hilly streets of Seattle just to sit in the middle of all that gorgeous splendor. There was a double feature playing. The movies were *The Parson of*

Panamint and *Shadow of the Thin Man*. Carole Lombard, Clark Gable and Marlene Dietrich weren't in either of them, but I was still looking forward to seeing both.

The usual crowd from my class was already there when we arrived. Barbara Andrews was the daughter of a policeman. She had long red braids that, today, were tied with green velvet bows. Sylvia Lindstrom, who had shoulder-length light blonde hair that Mrs. Rivington always compared to "corn silk," was sharing her box of chocolate covered raisins with Daisy Matapang, whose family came from the Philippines. Daisy's hair was tied back in a ponytail with a silk ribbon. Emi and I walked to school with all three of those girls every morning because they lived near us. Now we all settled in the same row.

I was surprised, and pleased, to see that two new faces had showed up at the theater – Vera and Maximillian Manteffel. They were the newest kids in the neighborhood and at our school. Vera had just joined our sixth grade class in October. Maximillian was in the seventh. They were a bit mysterious to the rest of us because they didn't speak very much English and we also didn't know them too well yet, but I liked them both.

Just like the movie star Marlene Dietrich, Vera and Max came from the faraway city of Berlin, the capital of Nazi Germany, over in Europe. The ruler of Germany was a maniac. His name was Adolf Hitler, and he was really and truly crazy. I had seen him on newsreels in the movie theater and they proved it. Hitler was usually shown screaming and yelling in German about something or other, with his face all screwed up and arms waving in he air. He reminded me of a baby throwing a tantrum, except he was a grown man with a Charlie Chaplin a mustache and a bad haircut.

It was hard to figure out why, but film clips from Europe showed Germans going gaga over the guy, saluting him by raising their right arms straight up in the air. Something about it, and him, gave me the heebie-jeebies. He was the guy who had started the war that had already been going on for two years in Europe. He'd already had the German Army invade a whole bunch of countries like France, Norway, Poland, Holland, and more, and even Russia, the biggest country on earth.

So I wasn't surprised to hear Vera Manteffel and her family had left Germany to get away from this Hitler and his regime. Quiet Vera hadn't told me about it herself, but it was no secret. I knew all about it because my father had interviewed her father, right after the Manteffels came to live in Seattle, for an article on "Life in the Third Reich" that was printed in the paper. The Manteffels were Jewish, and Hitler, who didn't seem to like much of anything or anybody he considered "foreign," declared that Jews, even ones born in Germany, were "foreigners," as crazy as that line sounded to the rest of us. I didn't get it at all. How could the German Jews be "foreign" if they were born right there in Germany?

I wondered sometimes what Hitler would think of a city like Seattle. We had a whole wonderful mix of people living here, from lots of different places and backgrounds, especially Asian ones like China, Japan and the Philippines. We all got along together, too. If someone like Hitler could see that, he'd probably pass out.

Vera's father had owned a store in Berlin, but because he was Jewish, the Germans closed it. "In effect, it was stolen out from under him," my father had written, "the Manteffel family's proud history of having owned their prestigious jewelry shop for more than fifty years wiped out overnight by a decree." It wasn't the only law against Jews. There were too many to count, Dad said. One was that Jewish people were no longer allowed to go to Berlin's parks. Another banned them from public beaches and resorts. Yet another expelled Jewish children from public schools.

"My wife and I decided we could not let our children grow up in such a place, subjected to one mindless indignity after another," Mr. Manteffel was quoted as saying in the article. He moved his family first to Paris, France, and then to New York. From there they rode across the country on a train to Seattle to live with relatives, Mr. Manteffel's Uncle Leo and Aunt Manya. They just happened to live on the same street as Emi and me, which was how my father met theirs. Leo and Manya had a lovely jewelry store in the center of town, near Nordstrom's, and had known my parents for years. When my father got engaged to my mother, the ring even came from the Manteffel's shop.

Max and Vera usually kept to themselves because their mother rarely let them out of her sight. Mom said after the poor woman had had to protect her two Jewish children from the Nazis while they still lived in Europe, she would probably watch over them like a hawk forever. Yet here they were, at the Fifth Avenue Theater, and without their mother.

"Well, it's about time you two joined the rest of us," I walked over and said to the brother and sister, giving them both a welcoming smile. "Ready to join in the fun?"

Shyly, Vera smiled back. Her dark chestnut brown hair was done in a sleek pageboy bob. It made her look at least thirteen, even though she was eleven like the rest of us.

Maximillian didn't smile, or at least, he didn't smile with his mouth, but his eyes lit up a bit.

"Join us and sit with us, will you?" I invited them.

"Thank you, yes," Vera all but whispered. Her "thank," with her accent, came out "sank." And she smiled.

Emi's cousin Nicky's sister, Molly Kimura, who was in the seventh grade like Maximillian, arrived next. She joined us, too. So did my classmate Lynnie Kinnatar, and her brother, Larry, a fourth grader. The eight of us took over more than half the row.

We saw more kids we knew, like Paul Yamaguchi, Tatsuo Gima and Christopher Callavari, also known as "The Three Musketeers" since they went everywhere together. All three were in my class. I waved at them. Paul waved back. I really liked good-looking Christopher but he never seemed to notice me, probably thinking I was "just some silly girl."

Then the worst boy from our school showed up. He was stocky, with straw-colored hair and a head so square it reminded me of a cinder block. At the sight of him, I let out a groan. Emi rolled her eyes. The boy's name was Jessup Marz, and he was never without his Chinese best buddy, Chester Yang, who was a head smaller and a lot slighter, trailing along behind him. I couldn't stand Jessup. He was a seventh grader who seemed to think he was a lot more important than he was ever going to be and it was hard not to wonder if he wasn't really from Mars with an S. I was happy to see the duo plunked their fannies down in another part of the theater, on the right, in the front, and nowhere near us. That was good. The last time my friends and I were seated in front of them they'd thrown buttered popcorn into our hair and called us names.

Max finally allowed himself to *really* smile when I offered him some of my popcorn. He shyly offered me some chocolate-covered raisins. He and Vera looked happy, but slightly shocked, that we had invited them to join us.

I was trying to figure out why when the newsreel started. Sometimes the newsreels were filled with real-life horror stories about air raids and bombings in England, ships sunk by German submarines, or Japanese invasions in Asia, but from the stories shown that day you would hardly know there was a war going on in many other parts of the world. The newsreel showed a livestock show in Chicago, Illinois, with a prize-winning cow and a dog who demonstrated how he herded sheep. A new cathedral was dedicated in New York. The newsreel mentioned the American armed forces, but only in terms of the Army-Navy football game.

"God bless President Roosevelt," I thought, "for keeping America out of the war this long, and making sure we're all safe here."

That was the last time I'd ever be able to say that to myself.

The Parson of Panamint came on after the cartoon, and it was better than I thought it would be, all about a decent preacher living among the phonies in a greedy gold rush town. Phillip Terry played the parson. But the main attraction of the day was The Shadow of The Thin Man. William Powell, who in real life had been Carole Lombard's first husband, starred as the husband of Myrna Loy. They played private detectives, Nick and Nora Charles. The duo of private eyes had a little boy and owned a little white Wire-Haired Fox Terrier dog named Asta. The plot involved a murder case at a race track. It was a comedy that managed to make the investigation seem hilarious.

We liked the two movies so much that we all stayed to see them again, even Vera and Maximillian, so the sun was ready to set by the time we emerged from the theater. Seattle was overcast most of the time, but that late afternoon the sky was clear. We could see the white snow on the slopes of Mount Rainier, the highest peak of the Cascade Mountains, in the distance. My gang trekked back home to our neighborhood in one big group, Sylvia, Barbara, Daisy, Molly, Vera, Maximillian, Lynnie, Larry, Emi and me.

Emi and I didn't burst out singing again as we led the pack home, but everyone started discussing songs. The most popular radio show, Your Hit Parade, would be on later that night. Recent hits on the show were "All of Me" and "I Don't Want to Set the World on Fire."

"I bet Hitler does," Emi observed of that second one. "Want to set the world on fire, that is."

"Or at least destroy London," I agreed.   England was the latest country Hitler was battling. He had his Air Force, the Luftwaffe, dropping bombs on England. We had seen newsreels of the bombardments with whole neighborhoods blown up, kids like us losing their homes. "Those poor Brits."

"Hitler already does – the bombs - to London," Vera said in her hesitant English.

"America's bound to be in the war soon, too, my father says," said Daisy Matapang.

"I know," I sighed. For more than a year, war was all the grown-ups seemed to talk about. Hitler's soldiers invaded lots of countries in Europe. Hirohito, the Emperor of Japan, kept invading ones in Asia. I didn't want to say so in front of Emi and her cousin Molly, but my dad kept saying the same thing about how America was going to wind up in the war, only if he talked about it when Emi and her parents weren't around he'd add that Hitler was only one part of the problem. Hirohito, Dad said, was another, and time would tell, but perhaps he was the bigger one. Mussolini, the leader of Italy, was the third, because he backed Hitler up, and who would want to be in league with Hitler?

Hitler. Hirohito. Mussolini. My mother said, "They can call themselves leaders all they want, but they're really just three stooges who want to take over the world. They couldn't care less who else is going to get caught up in the shambles they're making, either."

I was also going to have to pray harder than ever that night, and in church tomorrow, that President Roosevelt would continue to keep America out of the war.

Chapter Three: What's in the Cards

The December sun was fast setting, turning the landscape a deep shade of gold, when Emi and I said good night to most of the other kids, who lived on a different block. The only ones on ours were Vera and Maximillian. We four turned onto our street.

"Will you be listening to *Your Hit Parade* tonight, too?" I asked them, as Emi and I stopped first, since my house was the first one we came to, hers was next door, and theirs was further down the block.

"I have - not heard – before. But I - like to. What - ah, number?" Vera asked. Her English wasn't perfect yet. Whenever she talked, she stopped and started. That was the longest string of words I'd heard her say since she had arrived in Seattle and she'd already been here for two whole months.

"She means what station," her brother explained.

"It's on the CBS radio station. KIRO 710," said Emi, thoughtfully saying the numbers slowly in the hopes they'd be easier for Vera to understand.

Maximillian translated them into German for his sister, *"Sieben Ein Null."* Then he explained to us, "I just said 'seven one zero.'"

"Sev-ven. One. See-ro. I - tonight - listen," said Vera. Then she surprised us with the perfect American expression, "See you Monday!"

"Yes, see you Monday!" I said. "I'm hoping we'll all be great friends."

"*Ich auch,*" said Vera. "I mean, me too."

"Me as well. Have a good *nacht,*" Maximillian said, accompanied by his biggest grin yet.

"Night, not *nacht,*" Vera corrected him.

"Have a good night and a good *nacht,*" I said, so they wouldn't be embarrassed for slipping back and forth between the two languages, and they weren't. They were smiling big smiles as they went on their way.

"What a nice day this was," I said.

Then I saw whose car was in my driveway. It was a Cadillac. "Oh no," I whispered to Emi. "It looks like my father's old editor from the paper is here again, Colonel Barclay. He's retired now but spends time serving in the National Guard. That's where the 'colonel' comes from." The National Guard was the volunteer reserve army. "He's probably got his wife along with him, too. I'm supposed to call them 'Aunt Madge' and 'Uncle Reggie,' as if I'm their niece. Can you imagine? If I really *was* their niece I'd find some way to quit my family."

"Then mine would adopt you."

"That would be fun. We'd be sisters."

"It would be hilarious to tell people *we* were sisters and watch the reaction we'd get."

"Maybe we should try that anyway!"

It was never much fun to have Madge and Reggie Barclay visit, to put it mildly. Unfortunately they seemed to be coming around a lot lately. I wasn't eager to go inside, but a cold wind started blowing.

"See if your parents will let you come over to my house in time for the program, then," suggested Emi with a grin.

"And if they won't, maybe I'll have to escape through the first-floor bathroom window." I hadn't tried that move yet, but had thought about it the last time the Barclays had visited. Getting the window open wasn't hard and the sill was low enough to the ground for me to lower myself outside, nice and easy.

It was good to leave the bone-chilling raw dampness of the falling night and walk inside the bright hallway of my toasty-warm house, where a Tiffany stained-glass hanging lamp lit the rose-and-white-striped wallpaper, reflecting bits of reds, blues and greens onto it. Cozy.

The Colonel, who prided himself on still having a full head of wavy silvery hair at his age, was already holding forth at the dining room table, set, oh no, for dinner for five when I entered the house. That meant they weren't leaving for a while. "Out gallivanting around town on a night as cold as this one, are you, Ruby? It's going to be a wonder if you don't wake up with walking pneumonia," he grumbled in greeting, saying all that in a rush, where anyone else would have greeted me with a "hello."

"Good evening, Colonel. It's a pleasure to see you," I replied, lying about that in a polite tone because my parents always wanted me to be courteous to my elders. I didn't add the phony term "uncle," though. It was enough of a strain to claim it was nice to see him when it wasn't. The only pleasure for me came whenever I saw that man leave.

"Where were you, anyway?" his wife Madge demanded. She didn't bother to say hello, either, just fired the question me. She was a big woman, tall, wide, and square-jawed. Her salt and pepper hair was still standing almost straight up on end from the wind outside. Madge peered at me with narrowed little bright blue eyes behind thin wire spectacles. To top it all off, she had a loud booming voice. Where the Colonel grumped, Madge boomed. She sounded like a foghorn. What a pair! Why did my parents entertain these people?

"I was at the movies. Where else?" I replied. I took off my navy blue coat and favorite red beret. It was a present from Dad. He said with a name like Ruby it might be fun for me to always have something red on, like a trademark. I hung the coat and hat up on the wooden coat rack in the hall and sat at the table, quickly patting down my sandy blonde hair, which I wore in braids with bows, so I wouldn't look windblown like Madge.

Mom, wearing a nice dark green dress and with her shoulder-length auburn hair pinned up in the front, brought dinner from the kitchen on silver serving platters. At least we were having steak, peas and applesauce. I liked to eat all three. I just wished I didn't have to eat them with these two visitors present.

"At the movies, eh? With who? Your little friend Hirohito-etta?" asked Colonel Barclay. Then he let forth his trademark burst of a laugh, like he thought calling Emi a nasty name like that was funny. I bristled. Emi was nothing like Japanese Emperor Hirohito. He wanted to conquer the world with Mussolini and Hitler. The last thing Emi wanted was to set the world on fire. She was a good, fun-loving kid.

Emi knew that I didn't like the colonel and his wife, but I never had the heart to tell her my whole list of reasons why. The main one was that they didn't like or approve of *her*. Or, to be more specific, they didn't like it that she came from a Japanese family, and that I was friends with children from so many different backgrounds. That meant that they also didn't really approve of me, either. It was none of their business, but they never stopped sticking their noses in it.

"I was with *several* friends from school," I answered as coldly as I could, glaring at him, without naming them. That way I didn't have to specify whether I was or wasn't with Emi. Couldn't the Colonel and Madge go home? "We saw *Shadow of the Thin Man* and it was all about detectives solving a murder." Maybe I could get them both off the subject of Emi and onto another, like movies.

It didn't work.

"A *murder?* Frank," the Colonel said to my father, as I helped myself to some of the applesauce and peas, "I know it's probably out of line for me to say this, but don't you think young Ruby here really needs to befriend more children of her own kind, say by going to a Catholic school, rather than socializing about town in the dark of a December night watching murder movies with the heathen next door?"

I tried not to choke on my peas over that.

Dad replied calmly, "Colonel, there's also absolutely nothing to worry about regarding that child or her fine family. The Fujiwaras are our best friends, and – "

"Best friends?" Colonel Barclay exploded. His eyes looked ready to pop right out of their sockets. "What kind of *best friends* do you think *those* people are going to be if we get into a war with Japan?"

Mom kept her voice light as she answered him, but she was getting mad about what the Colonel was saying about the Fujiwaras. I could tell by the tight set of her mouth. "The husband, Hiroshi – Harry, we call him - was born in Japan, but has been here in Seattle since he was a small boy," Mom explained. "His father came to this country to work on the railroad during the last century, left a pregnant wife back in Japan, and sent for them right after Harry was born. He's as American as any one of us. He built the house next door and owns his business, too. Emi's mother, Noriko, is originally from Tokyo. Harry met her on a vacation trip back to Japan during the 1920's, and she's like any other American by now. Both of their daughters were born here, too."

"That doesn't mean your Hiroshi-Harry and this Noriko character have no overseas ties to that vile country," replied the Colonel as he pierced a big piece of steak with his fork, like he was stabbing it, "which could very well become *problematic* if we get into a war with the Japs. Besides, they can call themselves Americans, but only the children who were born here are. There's a law that prohibits that girl's parents from becoming citizens. In this country we don't give citizenship to Asians."

I had no idea what he was talking about. Mr. and Mrs. Fujiwara weren't citizens? And how could Mrs. Fujiwara not have ties to Japan when she was born there? She had plenty of them. She still heard from her parents and brothers who had never left Tokyo. For many years, Noriko's parents been sending Emi a beautiful porcelain doll for the Japanese holiday, Girl's Day, which I always thought American kids should celebrate too. One of Emi's uncles even sent her a valuable silk light green and peach-colored kimono to wear. I'd never seen such a stunning dress. And why would Mrs. Fujiwara staying in touch with her own relatives in Tokyo mean trouble if we went to war with Japan?

Nobody explained it.

"You've seen the headlines this week. Japan's been acting up, making threats, and driving our diplomats crazy. If there's a war with that country," the Colonel went on ominously, "who knows which side these Fuji-huji people would be on?"

"Fujiwara is their name, and America's not at war with anybody yet," I spoke up, struggling to keep my voice pleasant and not tell the old goat off good, though I wanted to, "so I wouldn't worry about it if I were you, Colonel."

"How can I not worry about it? Those awful Japs are a warlike people. They've been invading one Pacific island and country after another. They're as bad as the Nazis are and they're just itching to have a chance to get us into the war. It's so they can kill us all! Then once we're all dead they'll be able to come in here and take America over, easily. That's their plan."

"Really, Reggie! Not in front of the child," Madge all but whispered to her husband, yet it came out loud enough for me to hear. Even her whispers were like anyone else's booms.

I wasn't happy with that "child" term. Couldn't they see I was *eleven?*

"Did Emperor Hirohito tell you all of this personally, Colonel?" my mother could not resist asking. She caught my eye. There was a twinkle in hers, and I knew she was trying not to laugh.

"Of course not, but it's what's in the cards," the Colonel said. "You'll see! If the Nazis don't get us into it, the Japs will. It's amazing President Roosevelt has kept us out of the fray this far. I may get you into the service yet, Frank. I could pull some strings, get you into a good unit. And it would be better for you to join up than wait to be drafted and have to go anyway."

Now I was getting scared, not of the war, but of Daddy leaving us to fight. "You won't go, will you?" I asked my father anxiously. I wanted to hear him say no, absolutely not, that he wouldn't go away, ever, not even if he was drafted.

But he didn't.

"There is the possibility, yes, that I might join up if America goes to war," Dad said to me, trying to sound reassuring, "but so far, like you said, we're not in it."

"Yet," grumped the Colonel, "but you watch. We will be in it, any day now, and I'm looking forward to it, too! I'm in the Army reserves. I can hardly wait to go on active duty again."

Mom and I exchanged a look. Only Colonel Barclay would *look forward* to a war.

"At least the war in Europe has already created a lot of jobs here in Seattle," Dad said as a way of changing the subject to a more pleasant one. "I've been doing an article on how the Boeing aircraft plant's business has been booming since England's armed forces ordered lots of new planes from them. Our armed forces want to stock up on planes, too, so we'll have them at the ready just in case we do get into the war."

"We'll need them," boomed Madge darkly.

"We don't need them yet," I said. "In the meantime, could I go over to – um, to, you know, *my friend's house* – right after dinner to listen to *Your Hit Parade*?" I didn't want to mention Emi's name in front of the Colonel and give him a chance to make mean-spirited remarks about her again.

"Of course," Mom smiled. "But not until you've finished dinner and desert. Madge has brought us a chocolate layer cake."

"My favorite!" I smiled. Madge may have been an unpleasant character, but she had a talent for creating confections, as Mom put it. It was hard to like her, but I loved her cakes.

On the way out the door when I escaped a little while later, I heard the Colonel, once again, telling my father that I should not be socializing with "those Jap kids." This time he was even recommending I get sent to a private school where "no riff-raff" were allowed. Dad countered that by saying he was happy to send me to my terrific public school where I met "all kinds" of kids. Why my parents put up with those Barclays, I couldn't quite figure out.

* * * * *

Emi's house felt quiet and peaceful after that crazy dinner I'd just had with my parents and Colonel and Mrs. Barclay. Their living room was very comfortable, all in soft shades of light blue, mint green and silver. I loved hearing Emi's father explain how, in Japan, colors had meanings. Blue stood for purity and calmness. Green meant youth, nature and growth. "You are named," he once told me, "after a red jewel, Ruby. You would be considered very lucky in Japan. Red stands for good fortune, good luck. That is why our New Year's decorations always have red in them." I loved the idea of my name having thoughts of good luck built right into it.

Emi had learned to write in Japanese with ink and a paint brush at the Japanese school she attended on Sundays. Every word in the Japanese language was represented by a little picture character. Her family surname had a beautiful meaning. "Fujiwara" meant *wisteria field*. It was written in Japanese with two characters, one for the wisteria flowers, the other for a field. The first was a jumble of many curved lines, like the petals of a blossom, the second, straight ones, resembling a field with plotted lines. Last year Emi had painted the characters on parchment-like paper. Her mother had hung it on the wall in a gold frame.

On a side table there was also a little music box shaped like an old-fashioned gramophone record player with a gold horn. It played "The Blue Danube Waltz." I wound it up and listened to it before the show started.

I enjoyed listening to radio shows at Emi's house more than at my own. For some reason my mother didn't like it when I turned up the volume on the music shows. She was always nagging me to, "Turn that down! Turn that down!"

Emi also had a cute and very sweet little black Scottie dog she had named Buddy. He curled up on the couch beside me as we settled in by the radio to hear our favorite program. One of Emi's hobbies was keeping a record of the *Hit Parade* songs. She had a marble notebook used for just that purpose. Tonight she wrote the date with the pretty maroon fountain pen her father had bought her as a special present when school started this year. Her handwriting was pretty in English and graceful in Japanese, thanks to those classes she took at Japanese School. It flowed.

Mrs. Fujiwara entered the room and the delicate scent of her Shalimar perfume came along with her. She brought us Coca-Colas to drink as we waited for the program to begin. "I'm rooting for 'Chattanooga Choo-Choo' to be number one tonight," I said.

"I like 'Elmer's Tune'," said Emi. "They're both by the Glenn Miller Orchestra."

"We'll be on the California Choo-Choo soon," I reminded her, as though she needed reminding.

"Think I should bring some of my summer dresses with me? I know it's hotter in Hollywood than it gets here."

"I've been wondering about that myself."

"It may be good to bring both kinds," Mrs. Fujiwara suggested gently, as she rocked tiny Hanae to sleep in her arms. The baby's little head, which was just beginning to sprout a bit of black hair, poked out of a pink blanket with silk trim. "Some winter, more summer. You would be ready for any weather."

"Good idea," said Emi. "This is going to be such a swell trip!"

I reached over to the rocking chair where Mrs. Fujiwara was sitting to gently take hold of Hanae's hand. The infant was still wide awake, her little chestnut brown eyes, so dark they were almost black as an obsidian rock, remaining wide open. She was so little, smaller than my favorite baby doll, and I had loved her from the moment her parents brought her home from the hospital. I also thought her name was just beautiful. "Hanae" was Japanese for "blossom."

Mrs. Fujiwara felt her baby's cheek. "She is very warm tonight, yes? Too warm?"

I had no experience with any babies except for this one, so I had to admit I wasn't sure. "But yes, her hand does seem rather hot."

"I think she may have a fever," Mrs. Fujiwara said, getting up. "Come, Hanae. Time for a cool bath."

"Don't you want to hear the program, Mama?" asked Emi.

"Turn up the volume. I will leave the bathroom door open and hear it." How nice it was to hear an adult say to turn the radio *up*.

The show came on at seven o'clock, counting down the top ten hits of the week, beginning with Number Ten, which was a Glenn Miller band number, "Ev'rything I Love." He was my favorite bandleader, and Number Seven, "You and I," was another one of his songs. So was my favorite song at the moment, "Chattanooga Choo-Choo." It came

44

in as Number Three, beaten only by bouncy "Elmer's Tune" by the Glenn Miller Band in the Number Two spot and, at Number 1, a pretty but slow-paced number, "Tonight We Love" by Tony Martin. It had been Number 1 since the middle of November.

"I liked all of them," Emi said after the show ended. "Especially 'I Don't Want to Set the World on Fire.' It's still my favorite." It had been in the top spot but was down to Number 5 this week.

My father came by then. Mom had sent him over with some of the extra slices of chocolate cake that were left over from dinner.

I had to go with my parents to our Catholic church the next morning. Emi always went to Japanese school on Sundays. We said we'd see each other tomorrow afternoon, following dinner.

I told Mrs. Fujiwara that I hoped the baby's fever would go down. Then Daddy and I said good night to our friends and Dad walked me the few steps across the lawn back home.

I had no idea then, when I went home, took a bubble bath, changed into my cozy, powder-blue flannel nightgown, and settled between the bedcovers in my pink room to read a Nancy Drew mystery book, that in the morning, nothing would ever be the same again.

Chapter Four: The Announcement That Changed Everything

Mom and Dad woke me up at eight the next morning to go to church. My favorite time of the church year was Advent, the season of the weeks leading up to Christmas. This was the second Sunday of Advent, and there would be a special Advent wreath on the altar. There were four candles on the wreath. Three were purple and one was pink, and a new one was lit for each of the four Sundays. The first purple one had been lit last week, and the second would be lit today. By Christmas all four would be glowing.

We always dressed in our nicest outfits to go to church. I was still half asleep as I got into one of my best dresses, made from bright blue poplin material with a pattern of tiny orange-and-white flowers, and had put what my mother called "a nicer hat than your usual infernal red beret" on my head. Nicer? It was a navy blue round felt number with a small upturned brim that had a horrible bright green feather sticking up from it on one side, and I hated it, but Mom insisted that I wear that disaster on my head. It was more formal than the beret, that's all, but I loved the beret. There was a rule that Catholic girls and ladies had to wear hats in church. If I ever met the Pope I planned on telling him to get rid of that one.

After the service ended, Mom, Dad and I got into our car and sped off to a restaurant to get pancakes for breakfast. It was our Sunday tradition. The day was nice. Dad said maybe he and I could take a ride over to West Seattle later that afternoon and fly our kites by the Alki Point Lighthouse.

We went home right after a long breakfast that lasted until after eleven, and that's where we were when we heard the news.

It came over the radio as I was half-listening to a program on KIRO while sprawled on the floor reading about Little Orphan Annie in the funny papers. Suddenly the music program was interrupted by a news bulletin. The newscaster said that, according to President Roosevelt, the Japanese had attacked "naval and military activities" in Pearl Harbor, in Hawaii, from the air.

Mom stopped dusting the living room knickknack shelf to ask Dad and me, "Pearl Harbor? Where's that? Did they just say Hawaii?"

"Ssshh," said Dad. "Not sure. Let's listen."

For a moment, hearing anything further about the attack wasn't possible. The radio switched to a Jell-O commercial.

"It is in Hawaii," I spoke up. "Honolulu. I know it because Mrs. Rivington has a son in the Navy who's stationed there." Suddenly I felt very scared on behalf of my teacher's son. His name was Billy and she was so very proud of him that she kept his picture, in his white sailor's uniform, white cap and dark neckerchief, right on her desk. Mrs. Rivington was the prettiest teacher I'd ever had, and Billy looked just like her, only a male handsome version.

I asked Dad, "What does it mean by naval and military activities?"

47

"The attack is on our Navy ships and Army bases, I believe," my father replied, thin-lipped. He looked more worried than I had ever seen him.

Navy ships. Why in the world did Billy Rivington have to be a sailor in the very place where our ships were being attacked?

"Poor Mrs. Rivington," my mother murmured.

The news broadcast resumed. "There is no immediate cause for alarm and coolness will help us more than anything else," the radio announcer came back on, continuing. Then, maddeningly, what came on next but yet *another* Jell-O commercial, this one for butterscotch pudding!

"Oh, get to it!" My father said, irritated. Then he added a few choice words that were too foul for me to ever get away with repeating. They were all about what he'd like that radio station to do with their Jell-O.

I thought of the book of pictures Billy Rivington had sent to his mother so she could show my class how pretty Hawaii looked. It was a chain of flowery tropical islands in the middle of the Pacific Ocean where palm trees swayed in the breeze of the trade winds. It used to be a kingdom with a royal family, who even had their own palace, before it became part of the United States. What was happening there right now to our Pacific Fleet?

When the announcer was back, in time for another program to start, he said the attack was made on "all naval and military activities." I wasn't sure what that meant, exactly, but as the announcer went on and on, I knew that America's time of peace was over. This was going to mean war for certain.

The broadcast was continuing when a knock came at our front door. It was Mrs. Fujiwara, carrying baby Hanae. I let her in.

"Have you heard news?" My friend's mother asked me, looking frantic.

"Yes, it's horrible," I said. The announcer in the background was talking about the reaction to the attack on Hawaii in Britain. This was getting scarier by the minute, since Britain was already in the war.

"The baby is still sick. Burning hot. Fever. I called the doctor to make a house call, and was waiting for him when the news came. Radio said it is the Japanese who attacked. Emiko is at her Japanese class; my husband is at the ice cream parlor. I want to get Emiko but can not leave the house."

My father was already taking his coat off the rack in the hall. "I can go and get Emiko," he said. "A Japanese child shouldn't be walking the streets alone on a day like this. Noriko, by all means go home with Hanae and wait for the doctor. Mary, please, go with her and help Noriko," he said to Mom, "and Ruby, you come with me."

I grabbed my coat, forgot either the blue hat or the red beret, and raced to the DeSoto in the driveway.

"Did you get a look at that baby's face? Bright red," said Dad, as we backed out. "What a thing to happen at such a moment. Noriko hears our nation's under attack and she's got a sick baby, both. Turn on the radio and get KIRO, will you? Let's hear the rest of that broadcast, if they don't interrupt it to hawk more Jell-O."

We drove to the Nihonmachi neighborhood as quickly as we could without getting arrested for speeding, with the car radio continuing to describe the attacks on the harbor across the Pacific. A nearby Army Air Force base in Hawaii, Hickam Field, had been attacked too. This was bad.

It didn't surprise me to find Nihonmachi almost deserted, with no one on the street who didn't have to be. Several stores had already closed. A store owner across the street from the school was locking up as we parked. Then he darted down the street, pulling up the collar of his overcoat, as if he was trying to hide his face.

Dad kept the car idling at the curb. I raced inside the building to find Emi. I had visited the Japanese school only once before, when Emi was singing in Japanese in a show, wearing her light-green-and-peach kimono. I hadn't understood one word of that show. All the presentations had been in Japanese, but I'd been there to cheer Emi on. Applause is welcome, and the same, in any language.

A frantic Japanese gentleman who ran the place stopped me in the hallway. He looked startled to see me. I stuck out like a sore thumb with my light hair and slightly freckled face in the middle of a Japanese school. "May I help you?" he asked politely, though he looked frightened of me. Did he think I was a neighborhood ruffian, there to cause trouble after hearing the news of the Japanese attack?

"I'm a friend, sir. It's okay. I live next door to Emiko Fujiwara," I explained quickly. "Her mother Noriko sent my father and me to bring her home. We've got the car outside."

"Emi-chan is in Room 5," he said, using her Japanese nickname. "Which car outside is your father's?"

"The black DeSoto," I said, as I raced to find Emi's classroom.

By the time I found Emi and brought her outside, still struggling to get her arms into her coat sleeves, the man had talked to Dad, recognized he was Frank Rafferty the reporter, and asked him drop four more children off at their homes, all of which weren't far from ours. We squeezed into the car with the youngest two children, who were about six, sitting on my and Emi's laps.

When we got to the Fujiwara's, the atmosphere was tense. We waited for more news of attacks and the appearance of the doctor. I wasn't sure which was worse--knowing Hawaii was under siege or realizing we might lose this little baby doll of a girl that I adored who was boiling hot and so miserable. I held the baby as Mom and Mrs. Fujiwara took turns sponging her down with cool water on a washcloth. Hanae was usually such a content baby, but the fever made her cry and whimper. At one point

when the two mothers took a tea break I started to sing "When You Wish Upon a Star"

to her, gently, slowing it down as if it were a lullaby.

It was a long, tense three more hours before the doctor got there. I don't think any of us

were ever so happy to see anybody else in our lives as we were to see good old Dr.

Lindstrom, father of our schoolmate Sylvia, come up the walk with his black leather bag.

The baby had the croup, he said.

Soon I was dispatched to the nearest drug store on Queen Anne Avenue to fill the

prescription that would help her. Emi stayed in the house. Her mother didn't want her

to go back outside, and perhaps be taunted because she was Japanese, on this awful

day for both of our countries. Poor Emi. She looked down at their soft blue rug as

though she felt ashamed when her mother banned her from leaving the house.

I was glad to get away from it at that point myself, even though it was colder and

damper outside than it had been earlier. I was still in my poplin church dress and this

was a day for a woolen skirt. The streets were even more deserted, now that the news

had spread about the attack. It felt spooky to see how lifeless my bustling

neighborhood had become. Even old Mrs. Manning, who worked in her front garden all

year round unless there was a downpour, wasn't out. I couldn't wait to get the seven

blocks to the drug store and broke into a run as I covered the last three. The sound of

the string of bells jingling as I opened the door struck me as strangely cheery and

normal for such a scary day.

"Do you think Seattle will be next? After all, we're on the West Coast, too," a woman was saying to the druggist behind the counter, old Mr. Palmer, who still wore a handlebar mustache, as I waited behind her. She had short, frizzy hair with bangs, the color of steel, and one of those odd-shaped mouths. It seemed to turn downward at the sides and looked like an upside-down smile.

"Could be," our druggist replied with a nod. "The Japanese Navy seem to be the absolute rulers of the Pacific Ocean at the moment, and our city's built right on Puget Sound - an inlet of it."

Did he really mean what he was saying? That an attack was possible, right here in Seattle?

"Well if it could happen to Hawaii, it just as easily could happen here too," the lady agreed.

I started to shake.

Mr. Palmer noticed. "Ah, Ruby Rafferty, my good girl! Don't look so frightened, honey."

"But an attack, here!   That would be, it would be…I can't find words horrible enough to describe it, even though everybody tells me I've got far too much of a great big mouth."

The druggist and customer allowed themselves a small laugh.

"There's no planes flying over us dropping bombs on our heads yet," the stout lady said. She meant it to be reassuring, but I shuddered some more.

"Ruby, what brings you here?" Mr. Palmer asked me. "Nobody's much out and about today."

"I have a prescription to get filled, and it's urgent." I handed over the paper from Dr. Lindstrom. "Please charge it to Mrs. Fujiwara."

"Fujiwara!" the customer exclaimed. "Japanese? Oh, I wouldn't fill that one if I were you," she said to the druggist. "Let the Japs die just like they're killing us, I say!"

"Now, now, Mrs. Stenzel," Mr. Palmer appeased her, "we can't be like that."

"We sure can! My grandson is in the army. He's in training at a base in Texas but could just as easily have been sent to Hawaii, just like those boys who were murdered there this morning. That's what I call this attack, you know. Cold-blooded mass murder." She glared at me then, as if it were somehow *my* fault because I had come here on an errand for Japanese friends.

I looked this Mrs. Stenzel straight in her mean brown eyes, furious at her. "It's a prescription for a two-month-old sick baby," I informed her, "and I'm not leaving here without it." I was prepared to snatch it off the shelves, if need be. If I could figure out what it was, that is, because Dr. Lindstrom's handwriting was so sloppy that I couldn't read the name of the drug on the form.

"Ruby, you'll leave with it," said Mr. Palmer kindly. "Go have a soda at the counter while I fill this for you. It may take me a little while to mix it. Tell Belle behind the counter I said it's on me." As I sauntered away with my head held high like Carole Lombard in an onscreen outrage, I could hear him telling Mrs. Stenzel that she shouldn't say such things to a child like me or she'd be on every inch as bad a level as the Japs who attacked us that morning.

It was over an hour later when the liquid medicine had been created for Hanae. Mr. Palmer handed it to me and said he wanted to apologize for the horrible things Mrs. Stenzel had said earlier. "With a name like hers, Stenzel, of all things, she shouldn't talk. You can be sure the Germans will get into this war with us, just like the Japanese will, and Stenzel's as German a name as any I've ever heard."

"Don't worry about it, Mr. Palmer. You don't have to apologize. You didn't say anything wrong, she did." With that, I took the medicine and scurried through the eerie, vacant streets on the way back to Emi's house. Seattle had never seemed so quiet. Everyone with a radio was surely safe in their houses, glued to the broadcasts.

By the time I arrived, to cheers from Emi and her mother over the delivery of the medicine, Mom was still there, the radio was still on, my father had not come back from his newspaper office, and Mr. Fujiwara still wasn't home yet. "I'm starting to worry. Where can Harry be?" Mom whispered to me.

Molly and Nicky Kimura's mother called on the telephone just then. I answered because Emi and her mother were tending to the baby.

Mrs. Kimura said hello in English and continued in very fast Japanese. "Wait, it's me, it's Ruby Rafferty," I said into the receiver. "Let me get Emi's mom."

I called Noriko over to the phone. Whatever Mrs. Kimura was saying, Noriko, whose face had a naturally healthy golden tone, turned a pale shade of gray before my eyes as she listened. When she hung up, she said something in Japanese to Emi. After that she moaned, in English, "I could faint. This is so bad."

"What is it?" asked Mom.

"That was Hinako Kimura. She told Emi the FBI just came to her house. The FBI arrested her husband. She thinks they will take mine, too. Both own businesses."

"The FBI? Why would the G-men come and arrest either one of them over that?" I asked, using the nickname for FBI agents that I'd learned at the movies. G-men stood for Government Men.

"Because they are Japanese!" Emi's mother sounded about ready to panic.

"But that doesn't make any sense," I protested.

"Ruby, child, this is not a day of sense," Mrs. Fujiwara said in a gentler tone. "Hinako Kimura said burn everything Japanese. Like Japanese writing or pictures or, she said, anything, everything Japanese. The FBI searched her house and took away Japanese things. She said those make us look like spies! We look very bad to have Japanese writing they cannot read in the house. She said make bonfire of it."

"Spies?" I repeated, laughing. "In *your* family? That's crazy!"

"And a bonfire?" Mom added, shaking her head. "Oh, goodness gracious, relax. You've got nothing to hide, Noriko."

"Hinako said it does not matter. Burn it all. Fast! Before they come."

My mother took charge of bathing the baby again to bring her fever down even further than the medicine would as Mrs. Fujiwara and Emi ran around their house, looking for letters, photos, and anything else that was written in, or looked, Japanese that they could burn. There were lots of Japanese books. Mrs. Fujiwara brought armfuls outside and set them on fire. There were also letters from Mrs. Fujiwara's Tokyo parents and relatives. She sadly told me she had always treasured them, but they went up in smoke, too. The "Wisteria Field" sign Emi had painted in Japanese went next, right in the gold frame. I hoped it was only gold *painted*. So did a beautiful painting of cherry blossoms that I wished I could have grabbed and rescued before it was set on fire. Worst of all, when Mrs. Fujiwara came back in, she charged into Emi's blue and green room and announced that even the seven gorgeous porcelain dolls from Tokyo had to go. So did Emi's beautiful silk kimono.

"No!" Once again, that word popped out of my mouth before I could stop it. "No, please, don't destroy those! You can't. They're all too beautiful. Let me take them across the way to my room. I can hide them for you and give them back later, after, ah, the, um, FBI come and go." I still didn't think the FBI would actually come over here. The whole idea sounded completely nuts. Still, I figured the least I could do was to offer to save the dolls and kimono just in case they really arrived.

Yet I could hardly believe what I was saying. What was going on here? Why were we even talking about anything as strange as my having to help my best friend hide her *dolls* from the FBI? The Fujiwaras were just going a little crazy, weren't they? Surely no agents were about to come here.

"Yes, Ruby, good idea," Mrs. Fujiwara nodded. "Use the picnic basket to take the dolls over."

I found the Fujiwaras' picnic basket in a kitchen cupboard and lined it with the kimono. Then I put four of the seven dolls inside. There wasn't enough room for the other three unless I put them on top of the first four, and since their faces, hands and feet were all made of ceramic, that was a bad idea. I folded the kimono silk under and over those four, then raced out the side door of Emi's house and through the front door of mine, which we'd left unlocked.

Up in my own pink-and-white room, I had a chance to breathe easily for the first time all day since the announcement of the attack. I found my suitcase, opened it, and hid the first four dolls inside, wrapped securely in some towels from the linen closet. I momentarily left the kimono in the picnic basket, then ran back to Emi's with it to fill it with the last three.

"Here," Mrs. Fujiwara said to me, as I settled the dolls onto the kimono, "take these in the basket too. And thank you so much for this!" She put a bunch of photos of her family members into my hands. I let them fall gently on top of the dolls and was out the door again.

When I went back, everyone was smiling. Mr. Fujiwara had just come home safely. "Of all days to get a flat tire on the way home," he was laughing. It was getting quite dark outside by then.

Just as I ran over to him, about to give him a big hug, we all heard it. There was a loud, crashing tinkly sound, followed by shattering glass.

For a second I wondered if it was a bomb, and if Seattle was getting attacked now, just like Pearl Harbor.

But no. It wasn't a bomb.

It was their living room picture window getting smashed into a few hundred pieces.

A large rock, as big as a baseball, had landed on the carpet. There was a piece of paper around it, tied with a string. When we opened it, the paper said YOU FILTHY

JAPS SHOULD GO BACK TO JAPAN! A badly drawn skull and crossbones, the symbol for poison, was drawn beneath it.

Chapter Five: Invasion of the FBI

Everybody remained frozen in front of the shattered glass except me. I went flying out the front door without even bothering to put on my coat.

Two figures were standing on the sidewalk, laughing and slapping one another on the back, as if they'd just accomplished something wonderful. It was Jessup Marz and his sidekick, Chester Yang.

"What exactly do you two think you're doing?" I demanded.

They stopped laughing at the sight of me.

"Oh no," said Jessup, sounding sincere for once in his life, "did we hit the wrong house? I thought this was where that Jap Emiko Fujiwara lives."

"We didn't mean to hit your house by mistake," Chester added hastily. "We're sorry, Ruby."

"You *should* be sorry, you fat head, and you *did* hit Emi's house! I just happened to be over there. And I'm glad I was because now I'm a witness to what you just did! I'm going to tell the police and have you monsters arrested for this!"

"Let's get outta here," Jessup told Chester, starting to run, "come on! And *you*, Ruby! You're *nothing* but a Jap-lover!" Off they scurried into the night, like two big rats.

Daddy had always told me that if somebody didn't like what I was doing, my attitude in response should be, "Hooray for me – to heck *with you!*" So I replied hotly, "I'm a whole lot more than a nothing, and you two are nothing but *creeps!*"

"Ruby, get back inside the house," Mom called sternly from the porch.

"They should be brought up on charges!" I fumed as I slunk inside. "It was Double Trouble again," I said to Emi, "Chester and Jessup."

"I hate them!" Emi declared. "I've hated them since the time they threw popcorn into our hair and all over us at the theater and kept calling me a Slanty-Eyed Skunk!"

"Children called you that?" Mrs. Fujiwara asked her daughter, wide-eyed. It must have been the first she'd ever heard of it.

"And worse," said Emi with a shrug. "Lots of times. I'm probably going to get called even more awful names than that tomorrow when I go to school." She gestured toward the rock and the paper, still on the floor. "Now we're not just Slanty-Eyed Japs, we're the enemy, too."

"You're *not* the enemy," I assured her. "You're an American. Enemies aren't Americans, and enemies aren't eleven years old, either."

"Thanks, Ruby. But let's face it, right now I *look* like the enemy, no matter how young I am or where I was born. And does it matter to the two who threw *that?*" Emi asked miserably, gesturing toward the rock.

"I am afraid this war is going to make our lives a case of *tanzei ni buzei*," said Mrs. Fujiwara, then translated the phrase for Mom and me, "the few against the many. There are more people in America who are not Japanese than those who are."

"Don't be silly," Mom said, trying to reassure her, "nothing terrible will ever happen here."

"Mom," I sighed, "a rock just came flying through the window. It's already begun."

"Ruby, I'm going to call the police on the rock throwers. Are you sure you can identify those two boys?" Mr. Fujiwara asked me.

"Positive," I said, "Chester Yang and Jessup Marz. Unfortunately they go to our school. They're seventh graders. They're awful. I don't just want to talk to the cops about them. I hope I can get on the witness stand against them!"

Mom said with a nod, "You may have that chance, yes."

But the phone call to the police never got made. That's because that was the moment when the doorbell rang.

"Now what?" Emi muttered under her breath as she went to answer it.

Emi opened the door and froze in place. I was a step behind her and gasped to see who was on their doorstep.

There stood five G-Men from the FBI. Five honest-to-goodness G-Men! Emi's mother hadn't been exaggerating when she said she was afraid they'd come to the house. They were really *here*.

My eyes all but popped out of my head and stayed that way.

Emi jumped back from them. She moved to stand closer to her mother.

"Are you Hiroshi Fujiwara?" the leader, a fresh-faced man in a fedora hat with a booming voice, pushed his way past us, into the foyer, and asked Emi's father.

"Yes, I am Hiroshi Fujiwara," he replied, in as relaxed a tone as if he'd just met the agent at a party, although his eyes looked alarmed for a split second, right before he blinked his own watchfulness out of his expression. After that he kept his face blank.

"FBI." The agent flashed a badge, just like in the movies.

I was astounded to see this happening right in front of me, and in my best friend's house, yet. My mouth fell open.

So did Mom's. How could the FBI really be *here?*

The FBI were supposed to be the good guys. They fought crime. They went after bank robbers and kidnappers and murderers. Mr. Fujiwara ran an ice cream shop!

The agent continued, "Mr. Fujiwara, we need you to come with us for questioning. I'll stay with you while you pack an overnight bag." He gestured to the rest of the agents as he led Mr. Fujiwara toward the stairs to get some clothes from his room and ordered them, "Get on with it and search through this house! Make it snappy, too! We've got more Japs on our list after we bring in this one."

Emi jumped like she had been given an electric shock when he said the word "Japs." It was bad enough to get called names by rotten kids like Jessup Marz and Chester Yang, but a whole other type of awful when an FBI agent said it.

Emi's father called down the stairs to her mother, "Call Nicky! Ask him to mind my shop."

"No one," we heard an FBI agent roar at him, "is going to be running your shop right now. Like it or not."

It was just as Mrs. Kimura had warned Mrs. Fujiwara. The FBI had come to take her husband away. They started running around like crazy men on a hunt, pulling drawers open, looking under the cushions on the sofa and chairs, and looking for I don't know what. Within a minute of their arrival it looked like a cyclone hit the living and dining rooms.

One of the agents marched up to Mom and me. "What are *you two* doing here?" he demanded with scorn, like we were two pieces of garbage for being obvious-looking Americans in a Japanese house.

Mom replied softly but firmly, "We're their friends. We live next door, and I think you should know before you do anything else here that there's a very sick baby in this house. My daughter and I have been over here helping out. In addition to the baby, there's the eleven-year-old you just frightened as she opened the door. Both of those children were born here. They're Americans. Go easy on this family, for the love of God."

He sputtered at that. He was about to reply when I couldn't stop myself from putting my two cents in, too. "You can't take Mr. Fujiwara away! He's been here in America since he was little," I informed the man furiously. "He's one of us!"

"*We* can do whatever we want," the agent smirked at me, like I was an idiot. "We are in charge here, Little Girlie, not you. We'll decide who is and isn't 'one of us,' and nothing that's going on here concerns you. Now you and your mother need to make haste! Get out the door and go." He pointed the way out.

"Come on, Ruby," my mother said with the haughty grandeur of a film aristocrat, taking my hand, "let's not even dignify that with a response."

"Yes, sure we should go, definitely," I said as though I were directing my comments to Mom, but made sure they were nice and loud enough for that agent to still hear me. "How convenient for the FBI if we leave right now, this minute! I'd say they just don't want us to see everything they're doing to make a mess out of this house."

Mom was trying not to laugh at that even though she shook her head at me with a warning in her eyes to not say anything else. She and I grabbed our coats and, without even giving us a chance to put them on, the nasty agent led us to the door and ushered us out. Just as if nothing was wrong, and to bug the agent, I stuck my tongue out at him before he had the chance to shut the door behind us, then called over my shoulder, "See you tomorrow, Emi!" I kept my voice as light as possible, as if nothing was wrong, and as if I weren't steaming mad on Emi's behalf.

"Yes, see you!" Emi all but sang right back, getting into the spirit of not letting him get to her, either. Then the door was shut behind us.

Two agents were guarding their front door and yard. One looked us over, then shook his head at the other, as if to say he thought we were cuckoo for being over there at a Japanese house. I gave him a dirty look. I wondered if there were more agents guarding the side door and others at the back one, too, all preventing any possible escapes.

Why would the Fujiwara house have to be watched as if any of them were about to escape, though? This was nuts!

The rose-and-white-striped wallpaper of our hallway had never looked so inviting. We hung our coats right up on the rack since we'd never been given a chance to put them on.

Mom lowered herself rather wearily onto one of the lower steps of the staircase. She patted the dark red carpeting to get me to sit down beside her. I did. I found I was quite tired myself.

Mom suggested, "You might want to take a nice, warm bath while I fix us some supper. I just realized we've had nothing to eat since breakfast. I'll make us some franks and beans. I know you love those."

"That sounds good."

"I have never had such a day in all my life, Ruby."

"Me, neither. Would you put the radio on while I'm upstairs in the tub and let me know if anything else happens?"

"Of course. If I can rise up off this step, here, I sure will. War will be declared next, you can be sure of it," she said, stroking a stray lock of hair that the wind outside had blown too near to my eyes. "Maybe I shouldn't say this to you, since you certainly do shoot your mouth off a lot, but I'm proud of you for standing up for Mr. Fujiwara over there just now. Really proud. Those agents are completely out of line with the way they're behaving, tearing their house up like that and treating our friends in such a vile manner."

Before I could bring myself to go up the stairs, first I had to ask, "Why are the FBI even over there in the first place?"

"As near as I can make out," said my mother, "and as nutty as it will sound, they really do seem to be looking for Japanese spies. Or subversives. Or sleeper cells. Or *something.*"

"What the heck is a subversive? And what's a sleeper cell?" Both terms were ones I had never heard before, and they sounded evil.

"They're both alike, actually. A subversive is someone who is out to overthrow the government or a regime. An American-born person from a Japanese family could be a subversive, you see, if they were more loyal to Japan than to America. And a sleeper cell is a whole group of subversives, people loyal to another country who live someplace else, but are in position. They're spies or saboteurs, but they wait, 'sleeping,' in a way, until it's time to help their country. So," she sighed, "since today Japan attacked us, I think what the FBI is doing is trying to find out if Mr. Fujiwara is loyal to us or to Japan. They're trying to see if he's a subversive."

This was more confusing by the minute. "Well, if he was raised here, how could he be loyal to Japan?"

"Some people who have Japanese blood, born here, probably *are* more loyal to Japan. Maybe if their parents retained very strong ties to Japan, and their Japanese relatives, that could happen. Some of them might even really have become Japanese spies. Not all, but some. Take what happened today in Hawaii, for example. How would the Japanese pilots have known the very places to attack in Pearl Harbor this morning unless somebody had told them where America's ships were in the first place? You see? They had to have been tipped off on where to drop their bombs. So I think the FBI is trying to question some of our Japanese-born people here, in Seattle, to see if they can find out where they stand. Even so, it sure is horrible for them to take in a decent man like Harry Fujiwara." Mom shook her head. "I'm so sorry you had to see that."

"It's okay. At least I told that FBI man a thing or two."

"Ah yes," Mom laughed sadly, "you sure did. Though it might be a prudent idea to watch that great big mouth of yours when you're in the presence of federal officers."

"I would have - if they hadn't been acting like brutes. But they were. I ought to write a letter to President Roosevelt and report them for it."

"Where did I get you from?" Mom laughed. "You've got such confidence! I was a shrinking violet at your age. Still am. I was terrified in there when I spoke up to the FBI."

"But you did it, Mom. You were great!"

"So were you. You didn't even seem scared."

"Because I knew I was right," I shrugged, "and could see what they were doing was wrong. If you were so shy when you were my age, it's too bad you can't have a do-over of the sixth grade."

"I'd love one, but only if I could have you in my class with me to back me up."

"Since I wasn't born until you had me, that would be pretty much impossible."

"Even so."

I went up to the bathroom slowly, looking forward to a good soak in the bubbles. My throat felt a little sore and I was more tired than usual for a Sunday night. So far this had been the strangest day of my whole life.

But when I went into my room to get my yellow flannel nightgown out of the chest of drawers I smiled, seeing my suitcase, Emi's dolls' hiding place, was still on top of the bed. I was so happy to have rescued them, especially since the FBI really did come to raid the house next door. I made sure the latches were shut tight. The picnic basket with the kimono, family photos and the other three dolls was on the floor. I pushed both under the bed, way in the back, toward the wall. Then I put a few pairs of shoes in front of them for good measure. The FBI might be taking Mr. Fujiwara away, but no matter how hard they searched that house for Japanese items, I was glad to have made sure they would never, ever find these.

I tried to read my new Nancy Drew book, *The Mystery of the Brass Bound Trunk*, while sitting in my lilac-scented bubble bath, careful not to splash any water on the pages. It was a good story involving a boat trip to South America, but that night it was too hard to concentrate. Besides, I didn't want to miss whatever was being broadcast downstairs over the radio. I got out of the tub after only about ten minutes, too eager for the radio to continue with the bath, though on a normal night I could stay in there with a book for over an hour.

Snug in the nightgown, a pink quilted bathrobe, and my fluffy pink bedroom slippers, I padded down the stairs to the living room. I had just missed the evening news.

"We're not at war yet," said Mom, coming into the room with a plate of franks and beans in one hand and a glass of milk in the other, "but I heard that President Roosevelt will be addressing the nation at nine-thirty tomorrow morning. I think we'll hear something definite then."

"We should go next door later to see what's going on and if Hanae got any better."

"Not yet. I've been watching from the kitchen window. Would you believe it? The FBI is still over there! And no, don't you even think about looking out the window to make funny faces at them or do anything else in your misbehavior repertoire."

"Why not? They deserve a few. I'd even go turn the garden hose on them if only you'd let me."

Mom shook her head slightly and tried to say, "Absolutely not," in a stern voice, but then she smiled. "Ha, but wouldn't that be a sight to behold?"

The Jack Benny Show came on the radio that night, just like usual. I ate my dinner in the living room by the radio console. If it weren't for the fact that America had been attacked, the FBI was next door carting Mr. Fujiwara away, Dad was still at the newspaper office, and we didn't know what was going to happen next, this might have seemed almost like any other Sunday night. It just wasn't.

Chapter Six: The Yanks Are Coming!

I woke up, still with a sore throat, but decided to go to school just the same. I was too worried about Mrs. Rivington's son in the Navy who was stationed at Pearl Harbor. How could I stay home? I'd even had a bad dream that he had been trapped on a ship when the bombers came.

Mom asked me to be as quiet as possible while getting dressed for school because Dad hadn't gotten home until three o'clock in the morning and was still sleeping. He had done quite a few interviews the day before, speaking with regular citizens for articles to get their reactions to the attacks. Then he'd interviewed Colonel Barclay, now on active duty, others in the National Guard, the Chief of Police, and a hotel owner in the Japanese neighborhood. Finally he went back to the office and wrote about ten articles. I bet Colonel Barclay was doing a jig over getting recalled to active duty. Now *that* would have been noteworthy enough for a newsreel.

After breakfast I ran over to Emi's house, as usual, to walk to the corner where we always met up with Barbara, Sylvia and Daisy from our class. Several pieces of cardboard had been taped together to cover her smashed picture window. Emi wasn't up yet. Mrs. Fujiwara's eyes were red from crying. Her husband was no longer there. They had taken him away and he still hadn't come back. The house was a shambles.

"Emi is not going to school today," she said to me. "We want to find out where the FBI took Harry. I am not sure how, so I want Emi to help. I hope your mother will watch the baby for me. Hanae is much better this morning."

"Thank goodness for that much, at least," I said. Then I added, "Maybe Barbara Andrews' father would know where Mr. Fujiwara is. He's a policeman. Emi can show you where they live around the corner."

"That is a good suggestion, Ruby."

I had to dash outside so that I could meet the rest of my friends at the corner.

Daisy had gotten there first. She was facing in my direction, her shoulder-length black hair hanging loose today instead of tied back in a ponytail.

I was almost to the corner when Jessup Marz beat me to it. He came up behind Daisy, whose family came from the Philippines. "I'll get you now," he yelled, "Emi, you Jap!" Emi? Then I realized, from the back, Daisy's hairstyle resembled Emi's.

Jessup ran at Daisy. There he was, a year older, a head taller and a lot wider than Daisy, but he pushed and knocked poor Daisy right to the ground with a flying leap and a tackle. It happened so fast I could hardly catch my breath. Jessup held Daisy down, pulled her arm behind her back and started twisting it violently.

"Owwww," she screamed. "Stop it! I'm not a Jap!"

Jessup ignored that, and so did Chester, who came out of the bushes to join in what those two blockheads thought of as "fun." He slugged Daisy too, punching her in the back.

I ran to the corner to try to intervene. "Let Daisy go, you stupid louse," I roared. "Let - her - *go!*"

I got into the fray. I gave Chester a good hard shove. He wasn't much bigger than me, so that was easy. But then Jessup, who was taller and wider, turned on me. The thug shoved me off my feet. I landed facedown in a puddle of mud that stained my white socks a hideous brown. Both of my knees got scraped on the concrete.

I was trying to catch my breath long enough to let out an "ow" of my own, and then get back up, when something amazing happened.

Vera and Maximillian Manteffel had come flying down the street. Vera pulled Daisy back up on her feet and out of Jessup and Chester's way. At the same time Maximillian went wild. He landed a lot of punches. Jessup got hit several times in his mean-spirited face.

Jessup wasn't able to defend himself too well, not against Max, I was happy to see. "Stop it! Hey! Stop it," the bully whined.

"You stop it," Maximillian ordered, slugging Jessup one final time. "You have no *Ehre!*" It sounded like he was saying "air-ah." Then he realized he'd said the last word in

German and translated, "No honor! You have no honor if you are beating girls! Smaller girls than you! No honor! *None!*"

"I thought she was that enemy Jap kid Emiko," Jessup whined.

"So you didn't even look to see who you were beating up before your fists started flying and you knocked me to the ground?" Daisy demanded from the bully through her sobs. "How stupid can anyone be? I'm not even Japanese, you clod! I'm Filipino!"

"And Emiko's not your enemy, either," I told the two bullies. I rose off the ground to give Jessup a kick in the shins, using the foot with the muddiest sock. "Where's your brain, Jessup? I don't think either one of you has even got one. Do you fools really think Emiko was in Hawaii yesterday, bombing the harbor? She was right here in Seattle and you know it! You even have proof of it because you were here yourselves, throwing a rock through her window!"

"He did that too?" Maximillian asked, brown eyes wide, shaking his head.

"He's the most horrible boy in Seattle," I informed Max, "and yes, he did that too. His sidekick Chester here is just as bad, if not worse. He follows Jessup around like a dog."

"I do not," Chester protested.

"You do so. I'm amazed you don't bark!"

77

Vera spoke up then. "Daisy – hurt – bad."

Daisy told us she couldn't move her arm. "I think you broke it on me, Jessup! Are you happy now?"

"Jessup, you'll be murdering somebody next at the rate you're going," I said to him in disgust. "Even then you're so brainless I bet you'd kill the wrong victim. Get away from us! Can you walk, Daisy?"

"Yes."

Sylvia and Barbara came along at that moment.

"Then let's get you to Sylvia's house so that her father can look at your arm."

Sylvia said normally that would be fine but today it wasn't a good idea. "My father's been out all night, tending to one emergency after another. There's been lots of fights with Americans causing trouble for the Japanese. He's not home yet. Can you make it to school, Daisy?"

"Yes," Daisy replied in a small voice, since she was trying to stop crying, but without success. Her tears wouldn't stop. "It's my arm that hurts, not my feet."

"Let's get to school then and take you right to the principal's office," Sylvia said. "He'll know what to do."

We all loved our principal, Mr. Winbury. He was nice to us, not mean like I've heard some principals could be, and above all, he was fair.

Vera walked beside Daisy, holding her up on one side, not the one with the injured arm. I walked next to Maximillian. The two jerks, Chester and Jessup, continued on to school, too, but crossed the street to get off the same sidewalk. It didn't stop them from calling us names from across the street. They accused the Manteffels of being Nazis and yelled that the rest of us were Jap and Nazi lovers. "Japzis," Jessup sneered, "you're Japzis."

"Where did you learn to defend us like that?" I ignored him and asked Maximillian admiringly. "You were *wonderful!*"

Max smiled proudly at that. "In Berlin. Have you heard of the Hitler Youth?"

"I've seen them in newsreels, yes. Kids marching in uniforms, sometimes in torchlight parades, praising crazy Adolf Hitler."

"That's not all they do. The Hitler Youth liked to beat up Jewish children. Younger ones, most of the time. Smaller than they were, like my little sister. So I learned fast how to fight back. That's where I first start yelling about having no honor, too. To the Hitler Youth."

"It's a good line."

"The Hitler Youth talk a lot about 'having honor' but do not live like it. So it was an even worse word to use on them." He nodded in the direction of the duo across the street. "I do not think those boys understand what it means."

"You're lucky they understand anything. They couldn't do the right thing if their lives depended on it."

"Someday it might," said Daisy, hearing us. "Will they ever be in trouble then!"

"When it happens, I want a front row seat," I said.

Sylvia ran on ahead to school to find Mr. Winbury and tell him what happened since we were running late from the fight and the slow way we were walking Daisy the six blocks there. Mr. Winbury came outside and found us, wearing his overcoat, when we were a block from the school. He was as bald as Daddy Warbucks in the funny papers, just not as rich.

"Daisy! My God, what happened?" he asked her.

We all started talking at once. "Jessup Marz did it," said Daisy.

"Jessup and Chester struck again," I said.

"The same rotten pair as always," Sylvia put in.

"They are boys without honor," Maximillian roared. "They hurt Ruby, too."

I let the principal see what they'd done to my knees.

Vera didn't say anything. She just started to cry. "This – like – Hitler Youth," she said firmly to Mr. Winbury.

"Like the Hitler Youth! Jessup and Chester, boys from *my* school, compared to the Hitler Youth!" Mr. Winbury looked more upset than I'd ever seen him. "Wait until I get my hands on those boys! They'll rue the day. I'll see to that. Oh, Vera, Max, I am so sorry! How horrible it must be for you that they're reminding you of all that," our principal said.

"If the shoe fits," I shrugged. "They thought Daisy was Japanese, that's why they did this. The two of them broke one of Emiko Fujiwara's windows last night, too. I wanted to knock them out! Her parents were about to call the cops when the FBI showed up to take Mr. Fujiwara away for questioning."

Mr. Winbury gave a low whistle and said, "That's terrible. The FBI took Mr. Fujiwara, too? There are reports of Japanese people being taken in for questioning all over town. Meanwhile, something needs to be done with Jessup and Chester before they land in the nearest reformatory. For now, come on, let's get Daisy and you into school and to the nurse's office."

The nurse wasn't able to help Daisy too much, as it turned out. Mr. Winbury sent Maximillian off to his class, but since the rest of us were all girls, we went in with her and watched as the nurse got her sweater off, and then her blouse. "This child's arm has been broken," she announced, sounding horrified. "She needs to see a doctor immediately."

Daisy began crying again. "I'm not even Japanese, and Jessup broke my arm over it!"

"Of course you're not Japanese. Your family's from Manila," the nurse, who knew Daisy's parents, said kindly. "This is quite an outrage, and Jessup and Chester's parents will be hearing from the school about this. Meanwhile, let me see if I can help you get your blouse back on."

When she tried to get Daisy's broken arm back into the sleeve, though, the girl howled in pain.

"On second thought," said the nurse, "we'll just have to wrap your blouse and coat around that arm and try not to move it any further. Ruby, have a seat, hon."

Another child was brought into the nurse's office just as I settled onto a chair. It was a sweet little boy called Teddy Toyama. He was the tiniest boy in the first grade. His clothes were torn, his coat muddy, and his face and hands were all scraped up.

"Teddy!" Mr. Winbury exclaimed in alarm. "What happened to you?"

"Some man," the boy whispered, starting to cry.

"What do you mean, darlin'? What man?" The nurse asked, leaving me on the chair. She bent down to take a closer look at Teddy's face and hands.

"Some man. On my street. He asked wasn't I Japanese? I said yes. He pretended to walk away, and then came back up behind me. He punched me hard in the back and I fell down on my face."

"God Almighty," fumed Mr. Winbury, "a grown man did that? This can't be happening!"

"But it is," the nurse said. She shook her head. "Just hold your horses for a second, Teddy, and I'll take care of you next, as soon as I'm done with our Ruby, here."

"I have a feeling we're going to remember this day always," Mr. Winbury said to us, "and for all of the wrong reasons. What's happening is terrible. The Japanese and Asian children haven't done anything wrong, but this?" He said it like a question, gesturing toward Daisy, Teddy and me. It was one we couldn't answer. Mr. Winbury shook his head. "It's insane."

What kind of a situation would Emi be in when she came back to school, I wondered, if stuff as bad as this was going on?

"Jessup has no right trying to pull your arm out of the socket whether you're Japanese or not," I said to Daisy Matapang firmly, patting her hand on her unbroken arm. "Just who does he think he is?"

The nurse, meanwhile, gestured for me to sit down on the wooden chair she kept beside her desk. "Be brave," she whispered, "even though this will hurt a bit, so little Teddy won't be afraid when I clean his wounds up next." She cleaned my skinned knees with a potion that stung like mad, and then put bandages on them.

"That Marz brat ought to be expelled, once and for all," the nurse added to me under her breath as she applied them.

"Chester Yang too," I agreed, "his loyal follower who ought to know better. He's Chinese and somebody could just as easily mistake him for Japanese and beat him up."

"Don't give me ideas, or I'll be happy to slug him later on our way home from school," Sylvia Lindstrom fumed.

"Okay, girls, let's not have anyone else slugging anybody. First, I'm going to arrange to get Daisy's mother here so she can bring her to get medical attention," Mr. Winbury said when the nurse was done with me. "She's clearly got a broken arm. Teddy, I'll also call your mom to come and get you and bring you home, too. Then I'll be dealing with Jessup and Chester's mothers and fathers, too, to give them what for about what they're allowing their sons to do to people. Those boys will be expelled for awhile. Ruby, do you feel all right enough to stay for the day, or do you want to go home?"

My skinned knees hurt but weren't my only problem. My throat was hurting a whole lot worse, but I didn't mention it. I asked, "Will we be able to hear the President's speech this morning?"

"Of course," our principal said. "I'm calling an assembly about the attack on Hawaii. I plan to let the entire school hear the President's radio address in the auditorium. I also plan to address these incidents against you three, too."

"Then I want to stay." Oh, but did my throat ever hurt.

"All right, on to class with you, then, all but Daisy and Teddy," the principal said. "And keep your chins up, kids! This isn't America's first war, and it probably won't be our last. We've been through them before. Americans are great people. We'll pull together as a nation, you'll see, and come through this one with flying colors, too."

A lot of the Japanese students – we had nine in a class of twenty-five – were not there that day. Only three showed up. Paul Yamaguchi, who was one of the class clowns, was there, but unnaturally quiet. His eyes were puffy, as if he'd been doing a lot of crying. When I asked him if he was okay, he said in a voice not far above a whisper, "No, Ruby. I'm not. The FBI came and took my father last night."

I nodded. "Emi's too," I whispered. "Mr. Winbury just told us that's happening all over Seattle."

Mrs. Rivington was not in our classroom, either. I hadn't expected her to be. The music teacher, Miss Padegat, had been asked to substitute in her stead. "As you all know," she explained, holding up the photo of Billy Rivington in his uniform on Mrs. Rivington's desk, "your teacher's son is serving his country in Pearl Harbor. She stayed home today, hoping to receive news about him. I'm sure you all understand."

We did.

"If any of you would like to," she went on, "please take the next minute to bow your heads and say a silent prayer for Billy." Miss Padegat had no sooner said it than she bowed hers.

I bowed mine, made the sign of the cross, and said to God, "Please let Billy Rivington be all right. His mother's so nice to us. She doesn't deserve to lose her only son in this cowardly attack the Japanese made on our men when we weren't even at war with them."

Maybe it was due to the fact that Emi wasn't in school that day, but for the first time I let myself face the fact that the Japanese armed forces who had attacked Hawaii yesterday really and truly *were* cowards. It was one thing to side with my friend Emi and her family when they were being mistreated about the attack, but a whole other matter to think about Billy Rivington. Was he alive? Was he dead? What had happened to him at Pearl Harbor?

The Japanese armed forces were every inch as bad as Jessup Marz, I decided, attacking people who hadn't done one single thing to them and weren't ready for it. That made their actions against us yesterday seem pretty gutless, on top of being vicious.

Shortly afterwards we all lined up and filed quietly into the auditorium for Mr. Winbury's assembly.

It started with a salute to the flag. I had never fully felt the meaning of the words, "One nation, indivisible, with liberty and justice for all," in my heart before. Yes, I thought now, we're one nation, and let's hope we do become indivisible.

The whole school sang "The Star Spangled Banner" next with Miss Padegat accompanying us with flourishes on the piano. School assemblies always began with the pledge and the anthem, but today felt different. Every kid seemed to be singing with more feeling than usual, especially when we wrapped it up with the line at the end about how this was "the land of the free and the home of the brave."

Then Mr. Winbury got up to speak.

"Children, this is the one school assembly I wish we didn't have to have. We're living through some very difficult days," he began solemnly. "Our country was the victim of a surprise attack yesterday in Hawaii. The islands of Wake and Guam were bombed, too." That caused a murmur of alarm to ripple through the auditorium from those of us who hadn't yet heard more islands than just Oahu in Hawaii had been hit. "Last night, and this morning, there have also been incidents in retaliation here in Seattle against people of Japanese ancestry. This is not acceptable. It's disgraceful! I want all of you to know that, here at our school, our *fabulous* school where our student body comes from so many different backgrounds, I have always prided myself on how well you children get along. I am thrilled every morning when I come in here and see my students, with our roster of international and All-American last names, and how you're pals no matter where your families come from. We have always been a little united community at this school, and I want us to stay that way. Let the armies and navies of countries fight, but we must not fight with one another here!"

We all stood up and cheered. Every last one of us. Even me, although my throat and scraped knees still hurt.

Though some stood up faster than others. I could see Jessup Marz and Chester Yang, on the other side of the auditorium, sitting up front in the middle of a row between two of the school's toughest teachers, the boy's gym teacher and Miss Bryce, who had probably been told by Mr. Winbury not to let the two monsters out of their sight. They did stand up, but only after a long hesitation and a command barked from Miss Bryce. I could just imagine what she'd said.

Mr. Winbury announced that the President's speech would be broadcast in about fifteen more minutes, so rather than have us go back to our classrooms, he wanted to have an impromptu "Rally of Support" for our armed forces. Miss Padegat played one patriotic song after another at the piano and we all joined in, singing "You're a Grand Old Flag,"

"America the Beautiful," "The Battle Hymn of the Republic," and even "I'm a Yankee Doodle Dandy."

Once that one started, I wished Emi had come to school. We'd sung it as a duet in last year's talent show. We could have gone on the stage and led it. If my throat hadn't been so sore that it was making my voice sound faint, that is.

Vera, sitting next to me, was smiling and clapping in time with the songs. "Songs - I do not - know yet - but I like," she admitted. The whole assembly was on a rather hopeful note.

"Pal around with my friends and me, Vera. We'll teach you lots of songs," I promised her. She smiled.

Then the moment finally came. It was time for the President's speech.

Mr. Winbury had already hooked the rectangular table-top radio he kept in his office up to the loudspeaker system. When the speech started, it was amplified throughout the auditorium.

President Roosevelt was speaking not only to the nation, but to Congress, when he began, "Yesterday, December 7, 1941 – a date which will live in infamy – the United States of America was suddenly and deliberately attacked by the naval and air forces of the Empire of Japan."

Roosevelt mentioned even more Pacific islands that the Japanese had attacked yesterday than the ones we already knew about. Incredibly, after hitting Hawaii, Wake Island and Guam, they had also gone after Hong Kong, the Philippine Islands and Midway Island. How could they think it was okay to do this?

I thought of Daisy's family when Roosevelt mentioned the Philippines. Wow, was I ever going to tell Jessup off later for hurting her! Her family's country had been attacked just like ours.

The President talked a lot more about Japan. He wound up the speech by calling the Japanese attack "unprovoked and dastardly." I liked the villainous description.

Next came a Congressional vote. We listened to the entire roll call of both sections of the Congress, the Senate and the House, coming to us live from Washington, DC, over the airwaves.

"This, kids, is history in the making," Miss Padegat said. "And we're hearing it as it happens on the other side of the country!" Several children and Miss Bryce, my cranky old teacher, shushed her, wanting to listen.

Eighty-two members of the Senate all voted unanimously to go to war. It was an endless roll call, whether it was living history or not. Just as the Senate vote finished, the House of Representatives got polled next. I figured they'd all be in favor of it, too, but no, there was one vote against it. That came from Jeanette Rankin, the first woman elected to Congress. She was from Montana and wanted peace, not war.

It didn't matter. Three hundred eighty-eight out of three hundred eighty nine members approved. The majority ruled. America was now officially at war with Japan.

Mr. Winbury had Miss Padegat strike up one more song before sending us all back to our classes. "Here's an old war song that we sang when I was a boy," he told us, "when the United States finally entered World War I. We won that one, and I'm telling you, children, though we may have some tough days ahead of us, we'll win this one, too. The song's about letting the people of Europe know we were on our way there to help them out. George M. Cohan wrote it, and he's the same composer who wrote 'Yankee Doodle Dandy.' It's called "Over There."

The lyrics went:

Over there, over there,

Send the word, send the word over there -

That the Yanks are coming,

The Yanks are coming,

The drums rum-tumming

Everywhere.

So prepare, say a prayer,

Send the word, send the word to beware.

We'll be over, we're coming over,

And we won't come back till it's over

Over there!

Mr. Winbury sang it for us first, to make sure we would all know the words. Then the whole student body rose to our feet and sang it, over and over again, five times in a row, getting more pepped up about the idea of the United States of America winning the war by the minute.

Chapter Seven: The Ban

When I got home from school that afternoon, there was a flurry of activity taking place at the house.

Daddy was home from the newspaper office, although as soon as he said howdy he said he added he was going right back. "I just wanted to come by to help your mother put up the blackout curtains first," he explained. "Glad you're home, Ruby. The entire West Coast is going to be blacked out tonight."

"Blacked out? You mean, like they do in England so the Germans can't see the lights and know where the cities are to drop the bombs on them?" I asked. It had sounded creepy enough when I saw it in movie newsreels. I didn't want it happening here.

"Yes, and it means we can't let any lights be seen coming from any of the buildings in Seattle, or anywhere else. We have to cover the windows with enough material so no light escapes." There were several pieces of dark fabrics on the dining room table. He cut them with shears. One of them had been a blanket that used to be on the bed in our guest room. Some of the others looked like they were brand new, from a notions store. Sure enough, Mom said Dad stopped there to get them for her on his way home from work as soon as he heard about the new blackout regulation.

Dad cut, and Mom hastily sewed the tops into a flap just wide enough to fit a curtain rod through.

"These are going to cover our windows?" I asked, unpleasantly surprised. "They're so ugly! It's going to look gloomy from the inside. They won't match our rooms' colors, either." Our house was prettily decorated in tones of gold, pink, yellow and red, with only a touch of white and light blue here and there. The living room drapes were made of glimmery gold material with light pink roses on them. They were lovely. But my mother had taken them down. They were folded on the couch. Black material that didn't let any light in would soon be put up instead. It couldn't be worse.

"We can line the blackout curtains with prettier fabrics some other time," said Mom. "Right now, there's no time to gussy them up. We have to have them covering all of the windows in the house by seven o'clock tonight."

"Why so soon?"

"Because," explained Dad, "the authorities are saying there's a chance the Japanese Imperial Navy might have kept on sailing their ships this way, from Hawaii. They could be arriving on the west coast."

"Tonight," Mom clarified with a scared nod.

"There's going to be a radio blackout, too," said Dad. "There won't be any radio broadcasts at all this evening, but the plan is that one station, they say possibly KIRO, will stay open and come on the air if there's an emergency."

"Possibly KIRO? How would we even know which station to tune in to if something happens and they don't tell us whether it's KIRO or not? This is crazy," I shook my head and said. "It's all getting stranger by the minute."

"Welcome to wartime," said Mom, shaking her head.

I gestured towards the dark materials on the table. "Can I help?"

"Wars aren't known for their logic, Ruby. And you better believe it, you can help," said Dad. "Help your mother by stitching the top of that old blanket there which is being reborn as a curtain panel."

"But get yourself a snack first," Mom suggested, "and then come back in here to help me out."

As I went into our yellow kitchen to find some sugar cookies and spooned powdered chocolate Ovaltine flavoring into a glass of milk, I could hear my parents talking in the dining room with their voices lowered.

"Surely you can go back to the office now," Mom was saying, "since Ruby's here. She'll be more than able to help me with this."

"I know, she's a great kid. But I'll stay while we tell her the rest of the bad news."

"What a thing to happen," I could hear Mom say. "The girls are going to be so disappointed."

"We shouldn't have told them about it in advance, even though we knew their anticipation was going to be one of the best parts of the whole experience for them," Dad agreed. "Poor little Emi! She's all caught up in this now and she's not even a Japanese kid from Japan itself."

Hearing that made the sweet bite of cookie in my mouth suddenly become rather hard to swallow. *Now* what had happened?

I downed the Ovaltine and returned to the dining room.

Mom showed me how to sew the fabrics with an easy "blanket" stitch. "Don't worry about whether or not these stitches look nice. This is one time when it doesn't matter. The only concern is that the stitches hold so the lights inside of the house won't show."

I tried it, and Mom said I was sewing it just right.

Then she added, "Oh, there's one other news item, Ruby. And you're going to hate it, and your father and I really wish we didn't have to tell you about this one, but we do."

"What is it?" I didn't say I'd already overheard that it had something to do with Emi being Japanese.

"It's about Emi and the Hollywood trip."

"The Hollywood trip?" I repeated. I suddenly realized that for the past two days, there had been so much going on in the rest of the world that the trip hadn't even crossed my mind once.

"Yes," sighed Mom. "Oh, Ruby. We're so sorry about this. First of all, Emi won't be able to go. The entire Japanese population has been banned, as of today, from taking trains, buses, or driving out of the area."

"They've been *what?*" I repeated.

"Banned," said Dad. "It means they've been ordered to stay put. It's terrible, and it's unfair, but there's nothing to be done for it."

"Who's done the banning?"

Dad replied, "The government."

I couldn't believe what I was hearing. It was outrageous! "There must be some way around this!" I cried. "It was supposed to be *our* trip, Emi's and mine. *Both!* The Gemstone Girls were going to see Hollywood - *together*. I shook my head. How could anyone in the government possibly ban Emi from getting on a train? What do they think she's going to do, anyway? Blow Los Angeles to smithereens? For God's sake, she's eleven!" As much as I felt she and I were starting to grow up, and even though I hated

97

to admit it, we were still kids. Everyone else could see that. Couldn't whoever was making these rules?

Dad nodded. "I agree, honey. This is really nuts."

"It's not fair." I tried not to sob. It didn't work. "Why are they doing this?"

"There's a fear," Mom explained, "like I was telling you last night, that Japanese people who live here may be sympathetic to Emperor Hirohito in Japan. That they're working for him, not us. And, as ridiculous as this will sound about Emiko, that the Japanese are...enemies who are living within our borders."

"Emi's not an enemy!" I exclaimed. "Do they think she's some master spy or something, when she hasn't even gotten through the sixth grade yet? There's got to be some official we can ask to make an exception for her and let her go with us, or this is going to ruin everything! Who's in charge? Can't we complain?"

"Oh, no, honey. I don't think it's possible," said Mom. "This is serious stuff, what's happening here. Things are looking bleak. The Commander of the Navy even asked everyone today to be on guard in case we see anyone engaged in acts of sabotage. If we see it, we're supposed to report it. They think the Japanese are going to rise up and revolt against us, and that includes the Japanese who were born here."

"Mom, there's no way Emi would do anything like that," I declared. "Ever."

"I agree with you, Ruby. The government is being extra cautious, to the point I think they're going way overboard," Mom said, "especially when you consider they're even going so far as to prevent children like Emi from taking a trip on a train. Unfortunately, she's being lumped in with the enemy. Look, there's something else, too. Your dad and I have been discussing it, and we've been thinking that taking this particular trip to California at this particular time just might not be a good idea."

My eyes widened. "Oh, no! We're not going either?"

"Unfortunately. It's because of the threat of another attack," Dad explained quickly. "Los Angeles is a Pacific Ocean town, just like Seattle. Here at home, though, we may be living close to the ocean, but we're not right on it and we know our way around. There, if the place was attacked, and we weren't familiar enough with it to know which way to run, well, that could be extremely dangerous. I cannot put you and your mother in more danger than you might be in already. But don't lose heart. We still want to bring you to Hollywood one day."

"Preferably with Emi, too," added Mom. "But for now we think it would be best for us to postpone that."

"Are you all right with it?" Dad asked me gently.

"Sure," I said. It was a fib, and I don't like fibbing. I was furious at the whole situation, but what could I do when government decrees and wartime precautions were involved?

"That's my girl," smiled Dad. He picked me up then and twirled me around like he used to when I was little.

Then, as he put me back down, he noticed my knees with the bandages on them.

"Wait a minute here. What the heck happened to you?"

"Oh," I said, "Jessup Marz and Chester Yang happened." I explained the ambush of the morning, and how Vera and Maximillian Manteffel had been wonderful, coming along and helping the rest of us fight them off. "Daisy Matapang had to be taken to a doctor to have her broken arm set. I'm lucky I got away with scraped knees."

"*Lucky?*" Dad exploded. And they actually *broke* Daisy's arm? Those brats are way out of line!"

"Jessup and his crummy pal Chester mistook Daisy for Japanese. They got expelled for a whole week. Mr. Winbury threw them out of the school right after the assembly was over. I hope they never come back. They're awful! Say, can I go to Emi's after we finish making these ugly curtains and tell her all about everything that happened today that she missed?"

"It depends on what time we're done," said Mom. "The windows need to be completely covered by seven or else we'll have to sit here with all the lights out. The whole idea that the Japanese Navy might be sailing to Seattle scares me half to death."

"Me too," I admitted. "At least we don't live right by the harbor."

"I'll be home by about nine or ten," said Dad. "If I can. I hate to leave you both tonight. But there are so many stories to cover all at once. I may very well add another one about certain local brats who are running around beating up Asian children, too."

"Name names," I grinned, "if you do."

"Let me get those big blackout curtains up in the dining room first since those windows are our tallest. Say, why don't you two invite the Fujiwaras over to stay tonight? You can call it a slumber party. Noriko would probably appreciate it since Harry's not back from being questioned yet."

"Good idea," Mom said. "Ruby, run next door and invite them, but come right back, okay?"

I did, wondering about how Dad could talk about fighting the Japanese one minute and want to help our Japanese neighbors the next. I guessed it was because he knew the difference between which Japanese were the real enemy and which were trustworthy friends, something that Chester Yang and Jessup Marz would probably never figure out. It was terribly damp outside, more so than it had been when I had strolled back from school. I told Emi and her mom about the day at school, quickly, leaving out the fact that the boys who beat up Daisy mistook her for Emi. Once I got back to our house I had added a bad cough to a throat so sore it felt like it was on fire.

"I never should have let you go in today," Mom said, checking my forehead for fever, "since you've clearly gotten sick, and now you're worse. No school for you tomorrow."

"Hey, no school is always fine with me," I shrugged, or rather, all but croaked like a frog. I was getting worse fast.

If I hadn't felt so lousy, and if we weren't extremely on edge because an attack might actually be coming our way, it would have turned out to be a really fun night.

But I became hot with a fever right after all the windows were darkly covered and Dad went back to his office. I would rather have had him stay home with us. Mom made me sit in the tub in the hope of lowering my temperature. It didn't seem to help.

Emi, her mother and baby sister came over not long after 6:30, with Emi complaining loudly that she didn't like leaving her Scottie dog, Buddy, alone in their house if there was even so much as one chance in a hundred of an attack coming our way tonight. Her mother told her not to worry about it, since dogs were natural-born guards for houses. She settled baby Hanae on a big over-stuffed armchair, putting an adult-sized pillow at her feet like a border so that she wouldn't roll off. The little doll fell asleep right away.

The rest of us double-checked to make sure all the windows were well covered from the inside. After that, Mom told us to turn some lights on, went outside, walked around the house, came back and reported that I was possible to see a few glimmers of light from the very top of the living-room windows. Once she realized that, we decided to sit in the living room in the dark, lit by nothing but a pair of long white candles in silver candlesticks that Mom moved from the dining room table onto the mantle of our fireplace. Noriko also turned on a dim flashlight.

Mom brought Coca-Colas and ice cream for Emi and me, heaping more into my bowl than I usually could have handled since it was soothing to my throat. Mom and Noriko had pound cake and coffee.

I filled Emi in more fully on the day's events at school, but was more interested in her account of how she'd spent the day helping her mother try to find out anything about her father's whereabouts. "No one would tell us anything. We went to the police. We went to talk with Barbara Andrews' father at the police station. He said he didn't know where Papa was taken, and I believe him, but he was the only person who seemed to be telling the truth. Some of the others, I swear, Ruby, they were lying. They couldn't look at us when we asked questions and gave us really vague answers. We went to the offices of some politicians. We even tried to call on Mayor Millikin at City Hall, though we weren't allowed in to see him."

"Couldn't the mayor's office give you any information? You'd think he'd know. This is his city."

"You'd think it, wouldn't you? But who knows? I got the impression that the whole 'Japanese situation' as they're calling it is like some big top secret project no one can know about. What else can I think when no one will tell us where Papa is? Even if some criminal gets arrested for robbing a bank, his family is usually told where they're holding him. That's what my mother said."

"I've never heard of anything like this. Ever."

The whole time we were talking about Mr. Fujiwara I had to wonder if Emi knew that the Hollywood trip had been called off yet or not. Had her mother already told her we weren't going? I certainly didn't want to be the one to have to tell her. At the same time I didn't like the idea of keeping it from her, either.

At one point when Emi took the flashlight and brought our empty plates into the kitchen, her mother quickly said to mine, in a low voice so her daughter couldn't overhear it, "Did you hear? They have 'frozen' all Japanese bank accounts. We can not use our own money."

"Yes," said Mom, also softly, "isn't it terrible? Well, you know we can help you there if you're short of cash. And did you hear that there's travel restrictions, but only for the Japanese, too? "

"Emi does not know yet," her mother said with the heaviest sigh I've ever heard. "I hope they will be lifted before I must tell her."

"You do need to tell her, Noriko. Even if there weren't restrictions on her travel, we've decided to wait until things calm down, so it's postponed for awhile," explained Mom.

"Who's postponing what for awhile?" Emi asked, bounding back into the dimly lit room and bumping into the armchair on which the baby was sleeping. That made Hanae wake up and start to howl.

"Do not run so in the dark with the flashlight," said her mother. "Emi-chan, you do not want to fall and get hurt."

My mother quickly improvised, "Oh, they're postponing, ah, a movie starring *Carole Lombard*, honey. We were just saying we heard she wanted to be in some new movie and those Hollywood producer types are delaying it."

My mother makes a lousy liar. It was too dark to see Emi's expression, but Mom's voice sounded far and away too happy-phony when she came out with that silly line. I wished they would just tell Emi the truth. There was no way a kid as smart as she was wouldn't be able to figure out she was being told a lollapalooza of a lie.

I would have told her then and there but my throat was really hurting me. I didn't even want to sit too close to the others in case I was contagious.

My mother finally said we were all too tense and miserable in the dark of this particularly frightening night and started to sing Christmas carols. Emi and Noriko harmonized with her. I didn't feel well enough to join in, but it was fun to just listen to the three of them singing "Silent Night" and "Jolly Old Saint Nicholas."

Then Emi sang "The Last Time I Saw Paris," solo. It was a popular but sad song, all about how beautiful Paris used to be before it fell under the control of the Nazis.

"Do you think we'll be at war with Germany soon, too?" I managed to squeak, after she was done singing.

"Yes," answered Noriko with a small nod.

"I'd say it's inevitable," said my mother. "After all, they're in league with – " and she stopped herself right before adding, "the Japanese."

"It is all right," said Noriko with a sad look on her face. "You can say it in front of us, Mary. The Germans are in league with the Japanese."

Emi looked down in the direction of at the mauve rug on our floor as though it held her spellbound. That's what she did when she didn't like what people were saying. She looked down. Mom just looked away. I didn't know what to say so for once I kept my mouth shut.

We waited for bombs to fall or an army to land or whatever else might have been prone to happen in wartime if invaders were coming, but nothing did. The only frightening moment that whole night came at around eleven o'clock when, out of the vast silence of the neighborhood, we heard what seemed like a loud noise out back.

It turned out to be nothing more than my Dad, coming in through the back door, making far too much of a racket just by putting his key in the lock.

Emi was still worried about Buddy and asked Dad to go with her next door to get the dog. Once they returned with him everything started to feel a bit better. She, her mother, and the baby all went to sleep in our guest room. I was happy to finally settle down in my bed.

And Seattle wasn't attacked that night.

Chapter Eight: Surprise!

I spent the rest of that week staying home from school with a fever and all of the usual symptoms that went along with it, including a sore throat and stuffy nose, and did a whole lot of coughing and sneezing.

I wasn't comfortable at all, but Dad mentioned that if I had to stay home, it was definitely going to be an exciting news week. That was the reporter in him talking. He urged me to stick by the radio. I didn't have much of anything else to do except take the medicine that Dr. Lindstrom prescribed after making a house call and announcing that I had bronchitis again. I got it a lot. I drank lots of fluids like hot tea with honey or tall glasses of cool ginger ale. I ate a lot of cinnamon toast and Jell-O, reclined on the couch underneath a woolen blanket, and listened to as many music shows as I could on the radio. Sick or not, every time a big band show came on my mother started yelling at me to *turn that down!*

When I listened to the news, I felt happy to be home because chaos was breaking loose all over Seattle. For one thing, even though my city wasn't attacked on the night of the blackout, thank God, the day after it we heard there'd been a gigantic riot. People on a street in the center of town saw lights shining through some windows where blackout curtains had not been put up. They went berserk. Three thousand people were involved! They ran through the streets, breaking electric signs that were also strangely still lit and glowing like beacons for enemy aircraft, and even kicking in the windows wherever they saw a light shining through.   Dad said later the cops had their hands full trying to restore order.

That same day, Japanese language schools, including Emi's, were closed. The nice man who ran it, the one who had asked Dad to take the additional children home on the day we picked up Emi, was arrested just like her father had been.

At least 1,500 people were already known to be dead in Pearl Harbor. Dad said those were only the ones that had been accounted for so far. There would probably be a whole lot more. Where had Billy Rivington been when the fleet was attacked? I wished I would hear some news about him.

People, Dad told me, had begun saying the Japanese should be sent away for the protection of the rest of us.

By December 11th, the FBI was issuing warnings that "enemy aliens" – meaning the Japanese who were living in our country – shouldn't be allowed to have either guns or cameras. I knew why the guns weren't allowed, but couldn't figure out what was wrong with Emi or her parents having a camera. Dad explained that cameras were like weapons if they were in the hands of spies, who could photograph potential targets.

Spies, again.

Mom, at my insistence, went next door to retrieve Emi's new Brownie camera, the one her father had given her on the day we first heard about the Hollywood trip that she could no longer take. I got off the couch long enough to hide it in my room, under the bed with the dolls and the kimono, thinking again how nuts it all was. Then I went right back to the couch and the radio and drank another ginger ale.

The next news flash involved a strange fire in our area. It was said to have been set, *deliberately*, to "aid enemy planes." "Flaming arrows" had been reported, glowing on the ground. People panicked over that one, in the new usual way. The fear was that "enemy spies" had set fires deliberately, in the darkness of the blackout, to point the way to Seattle to Japanese bomber pilots.

The only problem with that theory? *No attack planes ever showed up!*

That same day Italy and Germany finally decided they'd declare war on America, too, to help their Japanese allies. Mussolini declared war on us first, Hitler second. Both wanted to support Japan. Hitler made another one of his notorious screaming speeches, ranting and raving against America. It was said to last 88 minutes.

Those three stooges who wanted to conquer the world, Hirohito, Mussolini and Hitler, were now standing together, united against my country. Well, we'd show them!

"That does it," said Daddy excitedly that evening as we sat eating dinner, or at least, Dad and Mom ate dinner while I had more ice cream for my sore throat. "If we're at war with the Nazis now, I have to, I simply *have to* get in there and help America win it! I knew they'd start up against us eventually. I've been in shock about their sick activities ever since the day I interviewed Rudolf Manteffel about what life was like for the Jews in Germany before they left." Rudolf Manteffel was Vera and Maximillian's father.

"No you don't," I tried to say. It came out too softly, my voice faint from having such a raging sore throat. I kept talking anyway. "Have to go."

Daddy didn't hear me. I couldn't have stopped him even if he had.

"I've been talking this over with your mother," Dad said to me, "and want to see if I can join the fight."

I looked at Mom. Was she going to just let him sign up? Unbelievably, she gave a slight nod. Things were getting worse. "Please don't," I squeaked. "Please, Daddy. Stay here. With us. Wouldn't you like to keep on writing about the war for the paper?"

Dad shook his head. "Oh, Ruby. I wish I could. But it's possible I could get drafted anyway at some point. It would be better if I join up now, as Colonel Barclay says, when I can have more of a choice in the matter, rather than wait, get drafted, and have to go wherever they might send me."

"You're going to listen to Colonel *Barclay?*" I all but wailed. "If that man suggested anything to me on any subject, Dad, I wouldn't listen. I'd run."

Mom laughed at that, but Dad was still looking at me in a serious manner.

"The guys from work," he said, "Marty, Joe and Fred - and I - are all going to the recruiting station after work tomorrow night to see if we can pass our physicals and get in. We want to all join up together. We're hoping to get into the Army. There's a training base not to far from here at Fort Lewis.

"The Army?" I repeated, like it was a question instead of a branch of the service. Armies were for soldiers. Soldiers could get *shot*. "Don't you understand you could end up dead if you're in the army? No! Absolutely not! Don't do this, Dad!"

How could all of these awful situations keep on happening? And so fast? The Japanese Pearl Harbor attack, rocks through windows, FBI arrests, getting beaten up on the way to school, Billy Rivington missing, war declarations, the Hollywood trip with Emi ruined, Hitler and Mussolini going against us too, and now this, all within just a few days. Everything was being turned upside down and inside out, nonstop and without letup. "You can't go. The Army is going to be so dangerous!"

"Wars are always dangerous. But the Army is a fine branch of the service, in my opinion," said Daddy. "The best. That's why I want to join it. Even your favorite old friend Colonel Barclay thinks so."

I made a funny face, all scrunched up, and said, "Just for that, if I were you, I'd join the Navy instead."

"Ah, just as we thought," said Mom with the beginnings of a grin. "We figured that since you're in the Carole Lombard Fan Club, not the Colonel Barclay one, you would try to talk Daddy out of joining the Army."

"The Army needs strong men like me. If I'm in the Army," Dad said, "and I can go after those Nazis, the war will be over a lot sooner. Don't you like that idea?"

"Well, when you put it that way," I had to admit, "I do. In fact, I don't just like it. I love it! If you must go, then go and kick their butts!"

"I fully intend to!"

On Friday night, December 12, when I was finally beginning to feel a little better, my father went, just as planned, to the recruiting office after work. He came home late, bringing his pals from work with him. They had all made it and looked so happy about that. Dad announced they were "thrilled" to be newly sworn in members of the Army.

Mom, anticipating victory for all four of them, had made a fluffy vanilla frosted cake decorated with an American flag made of frosting that she'd put on there with pastry tubes of red and blue icing. She had come to sit at my side on the sofa that afternoon, right before baking it, to say, "The gents are going to go off to war whether we ladies like it or not. We may as well encourage them and cheer them on."

"I understand it," I said, my voice sounding a lot better than it had been, more like mine than a frog's. "But secretly I'm not going to like having to do it."

"That's my good girl," Mom said, ruffling my hair.

"But you know, Mom, I don't just don't like this, I really *hate* this! Daddy could die out there on some battlefield, just like those boys did who were on the ships in Pearl Harbor. What's wrong with him *reporting* on the war? He doesn't have to go in it."

"You're entirely right, Ruby, on all counts," agreed Mom with a heavy sigh. "But he's made up his mind to go. Men all over the country are enlisting."

"Why is it that my father has to be one of them?" I grumbled.

"That's a perfectly good question. But he wants to do this, to join up and serve his country. He considers it noble. It's a matter of honor, not just our country's but his. If we're lucky, this war won't last too long and he'll get home soon."

Mom didn't say what could happen if we weren't lucky. I was already tired of the way the war kept on creating disruptions and we were not even a full week into it. What if it lasted for years? What if my father never came back? It was horrible to think about, but it could happen.

At least the cake turned out to be great, and I kept my promise to Mom. I cheered the guys on when they arrived, victorious. All four had successfully enlisted. I managed to keep quiet, though I secretly wanted to scream at the thought of Dad, Marty, Joe and Fred leaving Seattle to enter a training camp in Fort Lewis, near Tacoma. They were set to leave too soon - on Wednesday!

Dad had been buddies with those three guys from work for as long as I could remember. They came over most Friday nights to play cards and in the summertime, with their families, we met at parks for picnics. I was glad that if they had to go fight, at least they were going into the service together, but knew that if they went to war, it was very possible that all four of them might not return. Their joining the Army was the worst thing to happen yet.

I led them on a weak-voiced rendition of "Over There" anyway. What else could I do?

Billy Rivington wasn't found yet, Emi told me on Saturday night, when she came over to listen to *Your Hit Parade* with me. The blackout curtains had been fixed so that no light shone from the outside this time so we were, at least, not sitting in the dark, but in lamplight.

Billy was listed among the servicemen missing at Pearl Harbor. Mrs. Rivington had not been in school all week and Emi thought she was probably not going to be back on Monday, either.

I hated the idea of thinking of my teacher's handsome son might have been one of the boys who died. "It must be so hard for her, to not know what happened."

"I overheard Mr. Winbury talking with the art teacher, and he said she's halfway to a nervous breakdown over it."

"They'd better find Billy soon, and find him alive, so she doesn't have one," I said. "She's been my favorite teacher of them all, the way she's always telling us to 'hitch our wagons to a star.' I don't want her to leave us."

"Neither do I," shuddered Emi. "And I hope," she added in a whisper, studying the floor, "she doesn't hate me, or the rest of the Japanese kids, now, either."

"Mrs. Rivington? Never! She won't," I said, but thought to myself, you never know what people might do these days, since this war started. I hoped we could count on our favorite teacher not to turn on her Japanese students.

A new song had managed to get right up to Number 9 on the show that night, in its first appearance, immediately beating the Number 10 spot. It was called "There'll Be Bluebirds Over The White Cliffs of Dover." The White Cliffs in question, Daddy explained, were located in England. The song was about how much the British people, who were being bombed by the Nazis on a regular basis, were looking forward to peace.

"America's in the same boat as they are now," sighed Emi. She didn't seem like her usual happy self that night.

"Emi, what's wrong?" I asked.

Emi's eyes filled with tears. Then she told me how horrible her week had been. People on the street, total strangers, even some grown-ups, had pointed fingers at her, calling her "a Jap" and worse. A few of them had even used their fingers to stretch their eyes sideways and called her "Slanty-Eyes." Others took one look at her and insulted her, accompanied by making a mockery of Japanese accents, even though Emi didn't have one. Some of the kids in our school, ones she had always thought were her friends, like Barbara Andrews, were now avoiding her. She'd found out about those travel restrictions that were going to keep her from going anywhere, she knew our Hollywood trip was off, her mother was a nervous wreck, and her father was still nowhere to be found.

Dad heard her say that. "Oh, Emi, try not to worry too much about your papa. The authorities are holding quite a few Japanese people for questioning, sweetie, that's all. Rumor has it that there are Japanese business leaders being sent out of state to talk to the authorities and tell them anything they may know that might help the war effort. I'm sure he's safe and will be coming home to you soon."

I hoped he was safe, too, since he sure wasn't home.

I also wondered about what Dad had said. If everything about the FBI hauling Mr. Fujiwara away was really on the level, how come his wife and daughters hadn't heard from him all week?

Later, when Emi had gone home, Dad took me aside to tell me the rest of the story. "I didn't want to upset that good kid, but the authorities have Japanese men like Emi's father in jail."

"Jail? Mr. Fujiwara?" I thought of how nice he'd always been to me, my whole life, especially the day he gave Emi and me the Brownie box cameras. He hadn't had to buy one for me, too. I wasn't his child, she was, but he had given the cameras to us both.

Was he behind bars now? How could that be? Were they making him wear black and white stripes and eat bread and water? "But Dad, why? Does he even know anyone in Japan? He's been living here in this country for most of his life!"

"That's the worst of it," said my father, "yes. He has been. So far as I know, and I've known him since we moved to this house a month before you were born, he's never been in any kind of trouble in his life, but at the moment, it seems as if that doesn't matter to anyone who's in charge. On the other hand, if any of the men who have been taken away know anything, they do need to open up about it to help America. Now, we all know Harry Fujiwara, and we know he'll help America any way he can, so we shouldn't worry about him too much."

"Even though he's unfairly sitting in jail? Can't we do anything to help get him out?"

"Ruby, no. At the moment, I'm afraid we can't," said Dad.

"But there's got to be some way that we can! Mrs. Rivington is always telling us if we ever have a problem we shouldn't give up until we find a solution. There's got to be one for this!"

"Mrs. Rivington probably never counted on wartime measures when she said that, admirable though the idea is," Dad told me. "I'm not even sure exactly where the FBI is holding the poor guy at the moment. Wherever he is, I think the authorities will question him thoroughly, hear what he knows, if anything, then clear him and let him come home."

"Wouldn't they have let him out already, if they had? They took him on Sunday night. This is already Saturday. Tomorrow he'll be gone a full week. How long could asking him questions take?"

"Well, they arrested a whole lot of Japanese, so maybe they haven't gotten to Harry yet. Again, it's a wartime situation. He *is* from Japan and we *are* at war with that country, so this is a problem with a special designation."

All I understood was that the lack of sense to do with this war just didn't end.

I felt a whole lot better by Sunday, December 14th. I even left the house with my parents to attend church, where the pink Advent wreath candle was lit this week, and where Dad wasn't the only man to have joined the armed forces. A lot of them had already signed up. Even our aging priest, pink-cheeked, white-haired Father Murphy, said during the announcements after the service that *he* wished he were young enough to enlist. "In a strange way, in spite of the horror of the attack, I still think this is a great time to be an American, because we're all going to rise to the challenge and help the war effort, all of us, together, and do whatever we can." I liked that idea. "I know it's not just those of us who are too old to serve in the armed forces would like to join up. All week youngsters in this congregation have told me they would like to join the service, too." He gestured toward a third grader in the front pew. "Even Jimmy Quinn, over here, told me all he wants for Christmas is to be able to join the Marines."

That made everybody laugh.

"I'm too old to go, and Jimmy's too young, but that doesn't mean we can't find plenty of other ways of doing something to help. For a start, I'll be collecting Christmas gifts for our servicemen already serving in the Army at Fort Lewis." That was our nearest fort. "Army food is famous for being less than fabulous, so fruit and candy always work for treats for servicemen. Warm scarves and socks would prove useful for when they go into battle. All donations will be happily accepted, whatever anyone decides to give. If you'd like to participate, please bring gifts over to the rectory any time this week."

Afterwards Mom, Dad and I went out for breakfast, as usual, but it was to be our last one together for a long time. Next Sunday, Daddy would have already gone into the Army. We all realized it, and made that breakfast last as long as we could.

Later that afternoon the doorbell rang. Dad answered it.

Leo Manteffel, the great-uncle of Vera and Max, had come over. He was old and white-haired, about the same age as Father Murphy. I knew he had also come from Germany but not recently. He and his wife had been here, he once told me, for more than fifty years, coming to town so long ago that people had been driving horses and buggies. He had even come to my school once to tell the class what it was like when his tiny first store burned down in the Great Seattle Fire back in 1889. That fire had been massive. It destroyed twenty-five city blocks.

Leo told my parents he was there to see me.

"Me?" Usually he and his wife came over for coffee and cake with my parents.

"Yes, you, you wonderful girl," he grinned at me kindly through his wire spectacles. "You have no idea what good you did for my great-niece and great-nephew last week when you invited them to sit with your friends in the movie theater. That was their first time there, and though they knew all the kids here love going to that theater, they thought nobody would ever want to include them."

"Why on earth wouldn't we? They seem so nice," I said.

"They *are* nice. They're terrific children. But you see, Ruby, they got so used to being treated badly in Germany just because they're Jewish that they've been rather afraid to make friends ever since. Without even knowing you were doing something that to them would be extraordinary, you asked them to join in - and showed them they were just as good as everyone else. You even said you wanted to be friends. They came home that night and simply couldn't stop singing your praises."

"That's my girl!" said Dad, looking proud.

"Great work," smiled Mom.

"But I was just doing what anybody would," I protested. Still, I smiled, glad that by simply making a friendly effort to include the new-to-Seattle siblings, I'd done something really good.

"They both adore you like you wouldn't believe," said Uncle Leo. "Vera tells me you were out sick from school for most of the week. Are you feeling better now?"

"Yes, thanks."

"By any chance," he addressed my parents, "is she well enough to come to a little party we're having at my house tonight? It's the first night of Hanukkah, the Jewish festival of lights. We light special candles, the children play some games and we all eat a delicious meal. I came by especially to invite your daughter to join us."

I'd never heard of this Hanukkah before, but suddenly I wanted to go more than anything. "Yes, let me go," I said to my parents, "please?"

"I don't see why not," Mom said, "provided you're sure you're up to it. You're still coughing more than I'd like to see."

"I was up to going to church and breakfast," I reminded her. "Except for this morning I've been cooped up all week."

"Well, okay, then. Of course you can go," my mother thrilled me by saying.

"This is grand news," beamed Uncle Leo. "You know, when the children were home in Berlin, their parents used to host a great big Hanukkah party every year. They've missed all the fun they used to have there, before the situation got out of control with Hitler and his ilk. They haven't had a Hanukkah party since they left Germany, so I want to surprise Max and Vera with your presence there tonight. Don't tell them you're coming if you see them in the neighborhood today. Around four, their parents will be taking them out for a stroll while we get the surprise party ready. Just be there at five, okay?"

"I sure will! And I'm not planning on going outside until I go to the party anyway, so you don't have to worry I'll spill the beans." I really was still coughing too much, but didn't add that so Mom wouldn't change her mind about letting me attend.

"Should Ruby bring anything?" Dad asked. "A gift or something?"

"Just bring yourselves. Frank and Mary, you're invited, too, of course. Come as a family. Oh, and Ruby, would you know of any other children that I could invite?"

"Sure," I smiled, "there's Daisy Matapang, Sylvia Lindstrom, Barbara Andrews and Emi Fujiwara."

"Daisy's already on the guest list. Her parents came by to thank us and say our Max helped her and the rest of you when the local bullies were manhandling you. Emi Fujiwara – is that a Japanese child?"

"Yes," said my mother, "and if ever a child could use an invitation to a party, I'd say that child could." She explained all about how Emi's father had been taken away by the FBI.

Leo shook his head in sympathy. "That's terrible. That's the sort of thing that happened in Germany to the Jews, fathers being arrested over nothing. And over there, the Jews didn't even attack any harbors. Of course, Emi should be at this party, too."

"We'll bring her," my mother promised. "We can round up the Lindstrom and Andrews girls, too."

I called Emi first, who said she would love to go to the party. So did Sylvia, when I reached her. Barbara asked who else was going, and when I said Daisy, Sylvia and Emi, she got strangely quiet. "Sorry, but no, I can't go, and I've got to get off the phone," she replied in an unpleasant tone, like she was mad about something. Then she hung up on me.

I wasn't sure what that was all about. I called Daisy, too, asking her to walk over with us. She said her parents had also been invited, so, at quarter to five, Daisy, with her arm in a sling, her parents, Emi and Sylvia all met at my house to walk to the Manteffels as a group. I made sure to put my red beret back on before we left the house, rather than the navy blue hat with the green feather I'd had to wear to church, since wearing that thing once in a day was enough.

Daisy started singing "Jingle Bells." The rest of us joined in as we strolled over to the large house Leo owned.

He swung wide the door. "Right on time! Vera and Max and their parents are due back any minute. Come on in." He directed us to the hall closet first, where we hung up our coats. We entered the dining room, dimly lit by a crystal chandelier.

"Wow, is this place ever gorgeous," Emi, who had never been there before, whispered to me.

A large candelabra, made of silver and inlaid with mother of pearl, was on the table. It had room for nine candles. Leo's wife Manya was putting them in. "Just to give you some background on the holiday," she said to us, "it's a commemoration. Long ago, there was a war. It was another war where Jewish people were being treated badly, that time by a ruler called Antiochus. He was trying to stop us from worshipping as Jews."

"Sounds like something Hitler would do," I said.

"Exactly," Manya agreed with a smile of approval. "Well, it didn't work, of course. The Jews fought back. Their temple was vandalized by the army, and it took the Jews three years to get it back, but they reclaimed it. When they got the temple back, they only had oil to light the altar lamp for one day, but guess what?"

"What?" Sylvia and I asked in unison.

"It lasted for eight days. That's what. It lasted all the way until more oil could be brought to the temple. It was a miracle. That's why at Hanukkah, first we light the candle in the middle of this menorah," she gestured to the candelabra, "and then, every night for eight nights, we light another one. Miracles exist. And bad rulers don't last."

"Hitler won't either," my father said.

"Amen to that," said Uncle Leo.

We heard a key in the lock. It was the children coming home with their parents.

"Hold still, be quiet, and when they come in here, yell 'surprise,'" Manya urged us. She quickly turned out the chandelier light.

"*Kommen Sie in den Speisesaal,*" I heard Mr. Manteffel telling his family in German, and guessed he was probably saying, "enter the dining room," because that's what they did.

"*SURPRISE!*" We all sang out, just as Uncle Leo turned on the overhead chandelier light.

"We're having a Hanukkah party!" Aunt Manya told her niece and nephew merrily, first in English, then in German.

It was such fun to watch the expressions that played out on Vera and Max's faces. First, they had jumped, startled by the light coming on so abruptly in the dark room and all of our unexpected voices. Then they seemed astonished. After that they looked around as though they couldn't believe we were all there, and everything happened in the space of maybe two fast seconds.

Finally, they both couldn't stop smiling.

"A Hanukkah party?" Vera asked. "For us?"

"Like we had at home?" Max put in.

"Even *better* than you used to have at home," Manya assured them. "It's your first one here in your new home in America, the land of the free and the home of the brave. Everybody gets included here."

"If everyone gets included," Emi whispered to me, "how come I can't go on the trains?"

What could I say?

It turned out to be a terrific party. First we kids played a game with a spinning top called a *dreidel* that had four sides, each marked with a Hebrew letter. Uncle Leo – from that day forward, that's what the whole gang called him - had given us a whole pile of dimes to play with. Whenever my spin landed on a certain Hebrew letter, I could win a dime. If I got the wrong letter, I had to surrender all the dimes I won. I wound up with ten of them and was very happy since it amounted to a whole extra dollar I would be able to use to buy Christmas presents. Emi won twelve.

Vera made her final dreidel spin, then suddenly started to cry. Her mother, Rosi, who had been deep in conversation with my mother, asked her first in English, then in German, what was the matter.

Vera replied with one word, "Mitzi."

Max looked a bit sad when she said it, too.

"Mitzi Manteffel is our other great-niece, the children's cousin, their father's brother's child," Aunt Manya explained. "She was Vera's best friend in Berlin, too."

"No point in getting upset, now, children," Uncle Leo tried to reassure them. "You see," he explained to the rest of us, "we are not sure where Mitzi Manteffel and her parents are, over there, at the moment. They were trying to get out of Germany and go to Sweden. This was in August 1939. But we never heard whether or not they made it, and then all communication between Germany and the outside world basically came to a grinding halt once the war began in Europe that September. I've been in regular contact with a private detective in Stockholm to try and find out more, but so far, no luck. It's a mystery."

I was glad when my mother said, "I think that, no matter what religion any of us are here tonight, we should all say a quick prayer that Mitzi and her parents are safe, and that you get news of them very soon."

"Sounds good!" I agreed. "Please God, bring my new friends here good news of Mitzi."

"Amen," everyone chorused.

It put a smile back onto Vera's face, though Max blinked back tears, and then had to leave the room for a moment.

Aunt Manya announced that dinner would be served. That brought Max back. There was roast chicken, carrots, potato pancakes called latkes, served with applesauce on top of them, which proved to be a fabulous combination, and donuts filled with vanilla cream for dessert.

The Manteffels had a piano, and later we gathered around it. Vera, it turned out, had a great voice. She sang a pretty song in German that had been popular in Berlin. It was called *"Wenn du von mir gehst."* Her father explained the title meant "when you leave me."

"You should offer to sing that in the school talent show," my mother suggested to Vera when she was done.

"It is - not – English," Vera replied.

"So?" Mom shrugged. "I don't see why you can't sing it anyway, sweetie."

"Now might not be the best time," Uncle Leo said gently, "for her to be singing in the German language, what with Germany just declaring war on America."

"Some kids called us 'enemies' this last week," Max explained. "They don't understand. We left Germany because Jews are treated like enemies there."

"Did you tell Mr. Winbury?" Sylvia asked.

"It was on the way home from school where Mr. Winbury didn't see it."

"Well, Vera, you could always learn an American song, quick, and sing that instead," I suggested. "I really like 'Over There,' the one Mr. Winbury taught us in the assembly last week."

We all sang it, adults and children, together. Uncle Leo said he'd write down the words for Vera. I was getting excited about returning to school in the morning. It was going to be fun to be back in action and rehearsing for the talent show, especially now that Vera might be in it.

In bed later that night, I wondered where Mitzi Manteffel was. I added her to my prayers for Billy Rivington.

Chapter Nine: The Thing with Feathers

Monday morning I returned to school.

Emi wouldn't leave the house until her cousin Molly Kimura, who lived four blocks away, came over first. Molly had been walking with Emi all week. We met up with Daisy, Sylvia, Vera, Maximillian, and little Teddy Toyama at the corner. Since the day after he had been slugged by an adult, all the rest of us kids had been looking out for the little six-year-old.

All, that is, except Barbara Andrews. She was no longer allowed to walk to school with us, Daisy told me. Her mother had forbidden her to be friends with Japanese children!

Molly Kimura looked as miserable as Emi now did. Her father had also been taken away by the FBI when they went after Japanese businessmen. He owned a gift shop in Japantown. After she told me that, she said she didn't want to talk about it any further.

Sylvia asked me if I'd heard there was a big three-alarm fire last night at Pike Place Market. "They say it's the work of Japanese saboteurs," she whispered to me, so Emi, Molly and Teddy wouldn't hear. "Did your father report on it for the paper?"

"No," I explained, "he enlisted in the Army. He isn't with the paper any longer. He leaves for training on Wednesday."

"Wow, I wish my father would enlist, too, and be a doctor to our troops," said Sylvia, "but my mother doesn't want him to go. She put her foot down about it."

"Why can't my mother would act like yours?"

We found out at school that Mrs. Rivington's son had been found – *alive!* The entire class let out a cheer when we heard that. Some of the boys even started jubilantly singing a few bars of "Hawaiian War Chant," complete with hula moves, a popular number we'd performed in a school assembly back in September. We shushed them to hear more.

"Billy's safe in a hospital in Hawaii," the substitute said, "badly wounded, with a concussion and two broken legs, not just one, the poor kid. But the good news is the doctors say he'll recover." She was a jolly woman I knew from church named Mrs. Fitzpatrick. She always reminded me of illustrations I'd seen of Mrs. Santa Claus with her hair in a bun and her apple-red cheeks.

Mrs. Rivington would be coming back the next day, she told us. I felt my teacher's return would be the first normal thing that had happened in ages. Was it only a week and a day since Pearl Harbor?

I put my hand up and asked Mrs. Fitzpatrick, "Could we possibly make get-well cards for Billy?"

"And a banner," suggested Emi, perking up, "welcoming Mrs. Rivington back?"

There were murmurs of approval around the room. "Those are wonderful ideas. I would be happy to have the class work on them this afternoon," Mrs. Fitzpatrick said, smiling. "Meanwhile, Mrs. Rivington left word for me with Mr. Winbury that you're all going to be in a talent show early next week, and haven't had a rehearsal lately. So this morning, I'm taking you all into the auditorium to rehearse with Miss Padegat, who will accompany you on the piano."

Emi and I walked Vera over to Miss Padegat as soon as we entered the auditorium. "She'd like to be a soloist in the show, too," I told her. "Wait until you hear how she can sing!"

"Excellent," said Miss Padegat. "I am so happy to hear our shy little Vera wants to participate! Okay, Vera, what would you like to do?"

I thought she would say "Over There," but she told the music teacher that her Aunt Manya had come up with another idea the evening before, after the party was over.

"'White Cliffs - Dover,'" Vera replied, meaning the new *Your Hit Parade* song from England that was calling for peace. It was a brilliant choice for a refugee from the Nazis to sing. "If I may - read - the words – of – song – then I sing."

"Of course, dear. That would be fine. We'll put a music stand in front of you with the words on there."

Vera smiled. "Sounds good!" She still couldn't speak English too well but said that, I thought, just like an American.

"You're definitely on the way to becoming one of us," I said, and she beamed.

When I got home from school that afternoon, Mom asked me to go over to see Emi's mother. "She was hoping you might be willing to pick a few things up for her from the grocery store. Said she hesitates to send Emi out, what with all the hostility against the Japanese."

"Of course," I agreed. I went next door and got a list of milk, bread, cereal, eggs and a few vegetables. Mrs. Fujiwara thanked me over and over again for being willing to do the shopping. She wouldn't allow Emi to accompany me.

The world has gone so crazy, I thought. Emi and I went to the store for her mom all the time when she was pregnant with Hanae. Now Emi's father's in a jail cell and the rest of the Fujiwara family's afraid to go out of the house. Hirohito started this mess in Japan and good people here have to suffer the consequences.

I managed to get everything at a store several blocks away. It all fit into two heavy grocery bags that weren't easy to lug, but I was determined to get them to Emi's house.

I'd reached our block when out of absolutely nowhere, it seemed, Barbara Andrews suddenly jumped out in front of me, red braids flying, blocking my path. Her eyes, which were the pale blue of a robin's egg, were blazing mad, making her look ugly. That was strange, since she was pretty when she wasn't scowling like a librarian hushing noisy kids, the way she was now.

"Hey you!" she sneered.

"Hey yourself." I looked straight into her ugly eyes. "What are you doing, blocking my path?"

"What are *you* doing, is the real question," Barbara shot back. "Every morning, there you are! This morning you walked to school with three Japs, two Germans, a Filipino and Sylvia."

"Get away from me, Barbara! I've always walked to school with Emi, Sylvia and Daisy. So did you, until last week."

"Well, I don't now. You shouldn't either. Emi's a Jap. Molly and Teddy are Japs too. Max and Vera are Nazis."

"You couldn't be more wrong about Max and Vera! They left because the Nazis treated them badly, and – "

"Oh, grow up, Rafferty! That's what they're saying, okay? But is it really true? And if not, how would you know for sure? It's not like we can make a phone call to Europe to find out."

"Stop it, Barbara. We've all been friends for years and you know it! Except for the two new kids, but they just got here, and they're not Nazis. You get out of my way." She had to get out of my way, I thought. She was a full head taller than I was. Chances were I couldn't really fight her off if she got physical. Not with a grocery bag in each hand, and especially when one of the bags contained eggs that might splatter all over the sidewalk.

"No, I won't! Know what I think? I think the Japs in this neighborhood are all spies, and so are those Germans. And I think you're not a real American at all, either, because you're friends with them. You're nothing but a traitor!"

"You've flipped your lid!" I waited for some traffic to pass, then crossed to the other side of the street, trying my best to appear calm on the outside. I was shaky on the inside but determined not to let Barbara realize it.

"Traitor!" She kept yelling from across the road, as I continued on my way. "You're nothing but a traitor! A traitor!"

"You were our friend once, too, Barbara, so if I'm a traitor, then you're no better!" I shouted right back. "Think about *that!*"

This war, I thought, was certainly making a whole lot of people act ugly. At least I'd gotten out of Barbara's way so she couldn't force me to drop the bags and break the milk bottle or the eggs. Maybe a few of those eggs should have been cracked open right onto her head. Maybe I could bring an egg to school and do that to her at recess.

After I delivered the goods to Mrs. Fujiwara I ran home and told my parents, who were in their room, what had happened. Dad was busy packing a duffel bag of items like his shaving kit, toothbrush and toothpaste, some shoe polish, a few shirts and an extra pair of slacks, to bring with him into training. He wouldn't need much in the way of clothes because the Army would supply him with uniforms. I was steaming mad at Barbara and told Dad what had just happened.

"Pay no attention to that brat," Dad advised. "She has no right telling you who your friends are, or who they should be."

"She has no right waylaying you on the street, either," Mom fumed. "I'm calling that child's mother to complain."

The next morning I had to laugh when I saw Jessup Marz in the playground. He didn't look so smug any longer. He had a black eye. Rumor had it that he had picked on another Japanese kid whose brother was a champion on the high school wrestling team and slugged him one. "Ha, it serves you right," I said. "And if you ever touch me or any of my friends again, I'm going to give you an even worse black eye than the one you've got already."

Jessup Marz didn't say anything nasty in reply to that. He just looked down at the ground like he was embarrassed.

Mr. Winbury had not let him or Chester Yang off the hook over their actions from the week before. He allowed them back in school after expelling them for a week but their punishment didn't end there. Now they also had to help the janitor after school for an hour every single day for a month. Their parents were going to have to pay for Daisy's medical bills and the Fujiwara's front window, and were reportedly furious at their sons over it. Good.

The best news was that Mrs. Rivington came back! We had made two colorful, but mostly red, white and blue, banners for her the afternoon before. One said WELCOME BACK MRS. RIVINGTON. The other announced WE LOVE YOU AND BILLY, TOO! A whole pile of cards for her son were waiting for her on the middle of her desk. So was a bouquet of pink-and-white flowers from a girl named Annie Sanderson whose parents owned a floral shop. The whole class signed a greeting card to go with it.

Mr. Winbury, who was in on the surprise, kept her in the office for a few minutes so that we could set up the cards, banners and flowers. Then he walked her into our classroom. Naturally, as soon as they came through the door, the whole class couldn't resist all calling out, "Surprise!" Mrs. Rivington saw all of our decorations and burst out crying.

"Oh, what a great welcome back this is," she said as she wiped her eyes. "What a week I had! I missed all of you so."

"We were so worried about Billy," I said.

"And we're so happy he's all right," added Sylvia.

"Tell me everything," our teacher urged us. "All that happened last week! I want to know every single thing that I missed."

It took awhile to cover so many events. American kids told of relatives joining the service. Japanese ones reported their fathers and grandfathers had either been taken away by the FBI or were afraid they would be.

"So lots of American fathers, brothers, uncles and friends of students have enlisted in the service already," our teacher said after all those of us who had relatives who'd joined up had told her about it. "This is good. But lots of Japanese men have been taken away, too? That's horrible," she said to us, shaking her head. "I am so sorry I wasn't here last week while all of this was going on."

Barbara Andrews put her hand up. "I don't see what's so horrible about it. Everyone knows the Japs that were rounded up here in Seattle are probably spies and are working against us. They should all get out of here. And you should know that better than anybody, Mrs. Rivington," she added smugly. "Your own son was attacked."

Mrs. Rivington gave Barbara a long silent look. Her beautiful green eyes were not amused, but furious. "What I know," she finally said slowly, with ice in her voice, "is that the *Japanese armed forces* went after Pearl Harbor. And that not one single one of the children *in this classroom* had a father or uncle or brother who was there in Hawaii, participating in it."

I hoped that would shut Barbara up for at least a day or two.

"I would hate to see you children," Mrs. Rivington added, "turn against one another due to actions of governments or armies and navies, no matter what's going on. It's just what the real enemies of our country would like us to do, you know. They would like Americans to stop feeling united. Do you want to give Hitler, Mussolini and Hirohito something they *want*, during this awful time of war? And Barbara, I think you owe your classmates an apology for what you just said."

Barbara didn't say a word, just folded her arms, defiant.

"Barbara?" Mrs. Rivington prompted her.

She still wouldn't speak, but glared at our teacher.

"You can apologize to the class, or go and discuss this with Mr. Winbury, Barbara," Mrs. Rivington said with a warning in her voice.

"In that case, then farewell! I'll go see the principal," replied Barbara, and sauntered out, the dark green pleated skirt of her dress twirling as she hightailed out the door.

"She threatened me yesterday on the street," I told our teacher.

"She's turning herself into a tragedy," Mrs. Rivington said, "by doing exactly what the enemy would like us to do. I'll have to try and talk some sense into that child later. Meanwhile, we have a show to perform on Thursday night, and we need to rehearse! There's a new number or two we could add, for patriotic purposes. What do you say? Want to learn them?"

We all said we did.

As we were leaving that afternoon, Mrs. Rivington said it was important that we all come to school tomorrow for one final rehearsal of the show.

I put my hand up. "I can't. My father leaves for Fort Lewis tomorrow. Mom's keeping me home so that we can both see him off. I'm sorry."

"Don't be," said Mrs. Rivington. "It's all right, Ruby. You tell your father I said Godspeed until we see him again."

Barbara, who had come back to the classroom after a morning spent getting lectured by Mr. Winbury, mumbled under her breath, "*If* he does, not until." She was lucky Mrs. Rivington didn't hear it.

For some reason, after hearing Barbara say that, I found I didn't want to go home. Was it my father's last night before going to war, or was it his last night home with us, ever? What if that awful Barbara was right? What if, after Dad left, he never came back?

I lingered around the classroom after the others filed out. I offered to wash the blackboard for Mrs. Rivington. She said I should really get home, since the winter days were getting shorter, but okay, I could do the blackboard first. I went into the girls' room with the sponge we kept for that purpose and brought it back, just wet enough to do the job. Mrs. Rivington sat at her desk, correcting some compositions she had assigned us to write earlier. They were about everyone's plans for the holidays.

"Oh, Ruby," she said when she got to mine. "This is terrible! I've been so far removed from what was going on this past week that I didn't hear the Japanese aren't allowed on trains. So Hollywood is out for you, and Emi can't travel anywhere at all? You must be so upset, and she's going to be miserable."

"She already *is* miserable."

"You don't look so happy tonight yourself. Is it from the trip, Ruby? Or are you upset about this being your daddy's last night home?"

I put the sponge in the pail we kept in the classroom for it. "It's my father. Why did he have to enlist? My mother said I should cheer him on, so that's what I've tried to do. But what if I never see him again?"

"Oh, do I ever know how that feels, Ruby. You with your father, me with my son, it's all the same roller coaster of feelings, isn't it? We want them to serve, we're so proud when they do, yet we don't ever really want them to go. In wartime, there are simply no guarantees. I wish I could tell you there were, but I'd be lying. There are none. You can only pray for him to stay safe and hope. Do you know what Emily Dickinson said about hope?"

"No," I replied.

"She wrote:

'Hope is the thing with feathers,

That perches in the soul,

And sings the tune without the words,

And never stops at all.'

Isn't that a nice quote?"

I nodded. She had a quote for everything and they were always pretty good.

"Do you know what it means, Ruby?"

I shook my head. "Not really. Why would hope have feathers?"

"It's because if you have enough hope, your heart can feel like it's flying, like a bird taking off into the sky. So she calls it 'the thing with feathers that perches in the soul.' It's where hope lives."

"Would you mind writing that one down for me, so I can hang it up in my room?"

Mrs. Rivington smiled. "I wouldn't mind that at all. But once I do, you'd better go on home, my dear. Go home to spend time with your father tonight, and cheer him on as hard as you can tomorrow so you won't ever regret that you didn't."

She gave me the poem after printing it on lined paper. I went to the cloakroom to put on my navy blue coat and bright red beret. Mrs. Rivington hugged me before I left. "Even you're hat's like a ruby. See you on Thursday, my little Ruby gemstone."

It felt really good to be referred to as one of the Gemstone Girls again.

Chapter Ten: It May Not Calm Down

A nice relaxing evening with Dad wasn't what I got.

Dad's three friends from work, Marty, Joe and Fred, were traveling to the training camp the next day right alongside of him. All three were at the house when I got home, two with their wives, the third with his girlfriend. Mom had made another cake. Lots of other people came by, too, more of Dad's co-workers, the current editor of the paper, the entire Manteffel family, even Dr. Lindstrom, his wife and Sylvia. Dad and the other enlistees were pleased with the turnout. Mom forced lots of smiles but didn't fool me. She was going along with this whole army idea only because she felt she had no other choice. She should've been screaming, yelling and demanding that Dad stay home.

I was surprised when Christopher Callavari from my class showed up with his parents and big brother Carlo, who went to the University of Washington. Dad's colleague Marty was their uncle.

Only Emi and her mother and sister didn't stop by. I ran next door to get them, but her mother said no, they shouldn't be there, that it just wasn't appropriate because of their background. I said, "Don't be silly. Come and join us." I said it several times. But she wouldn't budge, so I ran back home to the party.

Colonel Barclay and his wife Madge got there just as the cake was about to be cut. The Colonel looked happier than I had ever seen him. He was back on active duty with the

National Guard and busy "securing Seattle," but had managed to get a few hours off to come say "goodbye and God bless" to my father and the rest of the newspaper guys he had once worked with. A thought crossed my mind that caused me to smile to myself. Maybe now that my father was joining up, Mom and I would, at least, get to see a whole lot less of the Barclays. That was the best thought I had the whole sad evening.

Meanwhile, the Colonel had brought several bottles of champagne along, and was proposing one toast after another to the "four brave men" who were going off to fight. Didn't he *ever* shut up?

I wanted to talk to my classmate Christopher but he stuck close to his mother and father.

All of the noise and activity at the party was starting to make me feel tired. I just wanted some time with my father, but I counted twenty-seven people in the dining room and living room alone, with even more behind the closed door of the kitchen. This going away party struck me as completely nuts. There was nothing to celebrate here. These four men might never come home, and there went the Colonel, raising his glass to them for the third time in the past five minutes!

Enough of this, I thought. They're all madder than hatters. Even a few seconds away from here would be better than staying to hear the next Barclay toast. I slipped on my coat, loaded two plates with plenty of cake and ice cream, and sneaked back next door to Emi and her mother.

"You didn't come to the party," I said with a forced smile of my own, "so the party is coming to you."

"This is swell," said Emi, "we got some of the cake and ice cream!"

Emi's mother, meanwhile, had tears in her eyes. "Ruby, you don't know how good a girl you are. But you are."

"You can still come over and join us," I suggested, hoping Emi, at least, would. "Though it's so noisy over there, I wish I could stay here."

"Stay overnight Thursday if you like, after the talent show," said Emi's mom. "You could have a sleepover with Emi like you used to before all this war trouble started. Tonight you belong home with your parents."

"It's more like my parents and the cast of thousands," I explained, making Emi grin a little, "but okay."

Back at my house, Colonel Barclay was in the living room giving Christopher's brother Carlo, of all people, a hard time. He was bellowing, "What are you, Carlo, nineteen years old? What's wrong with you for staying in that college of yours at a time like this? Your country needs you more than your college! Frank Rafferty enlisted, even though he's in his thirties! Why aren't *you* in uniform?" He was being more unbearable than ever, and to the brother of the boy I liked most in my class! I escaped into the kitchen for some soda pop.

After the Manteffel children, Christopher and his parents and brother, and Sylvia left, I finally slipped away, up the stairs to bed. Nobody noticed. The rest of the guests were still downstairs. Some were also smoking cigarettes, which set off my cough again. You would think my father and his buddies were going on a round-the-world cruise, not into a save-the-world war, and this was a bon voyage party. I couldn't stay down there one more minute.

I put on blue flannel pajamas, turned out the light, and got under the covers. No one, I figured, was going to miss me at the party.

I was wrong. I also didn't realize just how tired I was, but fell asleep almost immediately.

Awhile later, the door to my room swung open and the overhead light was switched on. "Here she is! I found her!" It was Daddy. He yelled that in the direction of downstairs, as if the party guests had been wondering what happened to me.

"Hi," I said groggily. I squinted in the glare of the light. It was too abrupt a sight in my eyes after having been sound asleep.

"Sweetheart, what are you doing up here in bed already? Weren't you enjoying the party?"

I didn't think it would be kind for me to tell my father exactly what I thought of that party. I answered vaguely, "It was okay."

"I don't suppose you'd want to come down and sing us a few songs?" Daddy turned my bedside lamp on, and the overhead one off. That was better. Less glare.

"Not tonight. Tomorrow?"

"Everybody will be gone tomorrow."

I didn't want to say "good." "Including you. Why in the world do you have to go, Daddy? Why can't you forget about joining up and just stay?"

"Ruby, I can't back out of it now. I've been accepted, and it's a great honor. Besides, I have a feeling this war won't last long at all. Thousands upon thousands of men have already enlisted. As the song you love says, the *Yanks* are coming! Once we got involved in the last world war it was over within a year. I think even though I may not be home for this Christmas of 1941, I'll be back in time for Christmas 1942."

"Well, now, that actually doesn't sound too bad," I had to admit, perking up at the thought.

"It won't be bad. America is going to be victorious! You'll see."

"I still don't want you to go so far away."

"I'll be back, even though I hate the thought of being separated from your mother and you. But wherever they send me, you and I will be always able to see the same sun in the sky every morning, and the same moon at night. They'll connect us in spirit until the day that I'm home. You can look up at them and think of me, and know I'll be doing the same thing, thinking of you. Good night, my little Ruby." Dad kissed me, tucked me in, and I fell back asleep listening to the sounds of the party downstairs, even as I wished the reason for it would go away.

I was up by six o'clock the next morning.

Party debris was all over the house, unwashed glasses still on the dining room and kitchen tables, dishes piled up in the sink. I took one look, and then went to work gathering up what needed to be washed and taking care of it so Mom wouldn't have to do it later. She didn't want Dad to go any more than I did. Today was going to be tough enough on her without having to do all those extra dishes.

I left them out to dry, then went back upstairs. Dad's train wasn't leaving until late in the afternoon. I took a bubble bath, then put on my very best winter dress, dark red velvet with long sleeves, a white lace collar and cuffs. It was, Dad always said when I wore it, a dress the very color of a ruby, and therefore perfect for me. I'd see him off wearing that one.

It was nearly ten o'clock when Mom and Dad finally got up. Both were thrilled to see that I had washed every dirty dish in the house. Mom put them away, high up on the shelves, while Dad announced he was taking "his last hot bath for a good long while"

since he had a feeling the training camp he was going to wouldn't have tubs, just

showers. I didn't want to cry when I heard that.

Mom said I looked beautiful and that it was a good thing I was in my best outfit. "We're

going out for one more nice, long family breakfast, kid."

The idea made me smile and lifted my spirits. I'd been so sure our last Sunday

breakfast after church would be our final one, and here we were, going off to the

restaurant again. "We'll be here together again one day," Dad promised, "right after the

war is over." I hoped with all my heart that he was right. It was still terrifying me that

Daddy might not come home alive. I hoped with all my heart the war would be over in a

year.

* * * * *

The train Dad and his friends were taking was going to leave from King Street Station.

Madge Barclay picked us up in her car and drove us, making me think I'd been wrong

the night before when I'd hoped we'd be seeing a lot less of her now. Mom had never

learned how to drive. It would be just my luck if she decided that now that Dad was

leaving, she would need *Madge* as her new best buddy, when Emi's mom Noriko was

her actual best friend, just like Emi was mine. Noriko, though, didn't drive either.

The red brick train station could be seen from several streets away because a tall clock tower rose high above it. I had always liked it, but not on this day. I felt worse about Dad leaving the closer to the station we got.

I was glad that, at least, Madge didn't come inside with us. She just dropped us off and bid my father farewell. She actually said the exact words, "I bid you farewell, Frank." Jeez! With that, she drove off. Mom and I were going to find a ride home with one of Dad's buddies' families.

Once we were inside the station, Mom hugged Dad, and that was the moment when she finally began to let her true feelings show. She started to weep. Dad told her to stop it. "Come on, that isn't necessary. I'll be back before you know it. Be strong," he told her, "for Ruby."

What had Mrs. Rivington said? All we could do for our family members in the service was pray for them and hope? Well, if these were my last few moments ever with my father, I wanted to look full of hope, not tears.

But they fell again anyway as his train was announced, and suddenly there wasn't any more time to say all the things I had wanted to tell him. I got one line in as we stood on the train platform – just one. "Zap the Jap" was becoming a popular phrase throughout the country, but I couldn't bring myself to say it because of knowing Emi. I settled on, "Clobber the Nazis, Dad, and then, come right back to us!"

"I plan on it!" With that, and a wave, he was gone, through the doorway of the train.

Mom and I, Marty, Joe and Fred's relatives, and other family members of other guys who were getting on the train to join the war, stayed on the platform until the train pulled out. We waved when it started to move. I could see Dad and Joe together at a window. I blew them a kiss, Dad looked like he was shouting something to us but we couldn't hear it since the day was cold so the window was closed, and I knew that was the last I would see of him for who knew how long.

"Want to go straight home, Ruby? Or would you possibly rather go to see a film instead? Maybe we could use a movie," Mom suggested. "I could certainly use a distraction before we go back to the house that no longer has your dad in it. We can take a streetcar or a taxi home later."

I wondered if she really wanted to see a film, or was just trying avoid going home. Either way, I liked the idea. It seemed like such a regular thing to go and do, and nothing had been normal since Pearl Harbor Sunday. "Yes, let's go." The Fifth Avenue Theater wasn't too far of a walk from the station, even in the cold, damp air. We strolled through historic Pioneer Square, in the first area of Seattle to get settled back in the 1850's. There was a Tinglit Indian totem pole there, and a wrought-iron structure called a "pergola" that, Dad had told me, used to be a shelter from the rain at an old cable car stop.

We also passed a store, a little further along toward the theater. It now had a hand-painted sign in the window proclaiming NO JAPS ALLOWED.

"No wonder Mrs. Fujiwara asked me to do a bit of food shopping for her the other day, rather than sending her daughter out or going herself," I shook my head and said to Mom, who was holding my hand as we walked along. "Look at that terrible sign! It's really bad for them."

"Yes, it is. They also still don't know where Emi's father Harry is yet, and still don't have access to their bank account to take out their own money. Can you imagine?"

"No, Mom. I can't. It can only get better for them, though, can't it? When things start to calm down?"

Mom gave me a concerned look. "This situation with the Japanese, actually, may *not* calm down, sweetie. Not any time soon. I want you to understand that things may very well get a lot worse for them before it gets any better."

"What do you mean?"

"I mean there's a lot of bad feeling against them, against the whole group. You and I, though, are not going to get caught up in that. We are people who stick by our friends through thick and thin, and Emi and Nori are our friends."

"Don't forget the baby, Hanae, too. And Harry, wherever he is."

It was a relief to get in out of the cold and enter the Chinese splendor of the movie theater. Mom bought buttered popcorn for us to share. From now on it would just be the two of us.

It was fun to be at the theater in the middle of the week, but I found it hard to concentrate on the movies. One was called *Small Town Deb*, with Jane Withers playing a teenage girl going through an awkward phase, and a mix-up over who would be taking who else to some big dance. It didn't make too much sense to me, but then I was thinking of my father on that train, moving farther away from Mom and me with every second that went by. I was also picturing Emi and the rest of the Japanese children in my class, having to walk past signs on the street against "Japs" every day, and them knowing they were the people it was directed against, just like Vera and Max Manteffel had once had to walk past signs against Jews when they still lived in Germany. Jews there still had to endure that kind of meanness, still knew every day they were being left out. It was getting hard to imagine the silly little problems people were having in the movie, where a date for a dance was turned into a major catastrophe, when real ones seemed to be happening all the time.

The next movie at the double feature was yet another movie about a reverend, like *The Parson of Panamint*, this one called *One Foot in Heaven*. Frederic March played the minister. He and his family moved around a lot, going along with him from his job at one church to another.

Too bad the Army didn't let families go with their fathers, too, I thought. Though it would have been easier to live with a minister who got to stay put than an Army man who had to go forth and conquer.

Chapter Eleven: Loud and Strong

Emi gave me the news about the talent show the next morning as we walked to school. "Mrs. Rivington thinks we should sing different songs. Not 'Glow Worm' and the one about the bumble bee."

"What? That's crazy! The show is tonight, and those are the numbers we've been rehearsing all this time."

"I know, but she thinks it might be a good idea for us to sing something more patriotic instead."

"Like what?"

"She suggested 'You're A Grand Old Flag.'"

"Well, at least we know it already." We waited at the corner for Daisy, Sylvia, Vera, Max and Teddy to join us and I started to sing:

"You're a grand old flag,
You're a high-flying flag,
And forever in peace may you wave…"

I stopped right there. "It wouldn't make sense to sing that one. The flag isn't flying in peace right now."

"Never thought of it when she suggested it, but you're right," Emi agreed.

"We should just sing what we planned. The songs may not be patriotic but they're perfectly nice and we know them well already."

"I'm glad you said that," Emi gave a little smile of relief. "I didn't really want to rehearse a new number at the last minute, either."

"Mrs. Rivington," I said, "doesn't seem like the type who'd force us to change it. Let's tell her we really don't want to and see what she says."

Mrs. Rivington said she was fine with our not changing the song, but I wondered. She may have said with her mouth that it was okay with her, but her eyes looked oddly worried about something that she didn't express.

And then I figured it out. She was concerned about a duet by an "American" kid and her "Japanese" friend. People these days were being so cruel.

Max and Vera's mother Rosi was having a cup of tea with Mom when I got home from school. She had gone to college in England and had no problem speaking our language. Rosi and Mom had really hit it off when they met at the Hanukkah party. They'd been talking, but stopped abruptly and went silent as soon as I entered the kitchen.

Too silent. I'd obviously caught them discussing something they didn't want me to hear.

I didn't like that. Something else had to be wrong. "What's the matter?" I asked Mom anxiously.

"Nothing. Why would anything be the matter?"

"Something must be. Why else would you stop talking in the middle of your sentence?" Didn't she realize that it frightened me? Especially these days.

"Don't be silly," Mom said.

"I'm not. What aren't you telling me?" My worst fear came out of my mouth before I could stop it. "Did something happen to Dad's train?"

"What?" Mom repeated. "Oh, heavens, no, Ruby! It's just, haven't you heard? When it's this close to Christmas, 'tis not the season to ask your elders questions." Mom winked. "That's why parents sometimes stop talking in December when their kids enter rooms, sweetie, even during wartime."

"I'd almost forgotten about Christmas," I admitted, letting out the breath I hadn't realized I'd been holding. "Well, thank goodness it's not about Dad."

"The children," Mrs. Manteffel sighed, "they get the worst of it in times like these. Growing up so worried. My two are more like thirty-year-olds, but both have yet to reach age thirteen." She got up from her chair to leave. "Well, I am looking forward to seeing you perform tonight, Ruby. Try not to worry about your papa too much. It does not help."

The show was that night at seven o'clock sharp. Emi and I had to report to our classroom first, before going to the backstage area of the auditorium. Mrs. Rivington said when we entered, "There you two are! Are you ready for your big debut as 'The Gemstone Girls?'"

"We sure are," I said.

"Yes," agreed Emi, but suddenly she didn't look as sure of herself as she usually did.

I was glad my mother was there to see the show, even though I felt really bad that Daddy wasn't. I wondered what he was doing right now at the fort. Was he in uniform yet? Learning to march? Shooting a gun on a rifle range?

The show started with the pledge to the flag. The entire auditorium, parents too, stood, recited the pledge, and sang the national anthem. Then my whole class, standing on risers, sang the opening number we had planned on using before the war began, which was "Roll Out the Barrel." After that, we swung into "When You Wish Upon a Star" and "Puttin' on the Ritz." Miss Padegat outdid herself with her piano accompaniment.

Three boys dressed as soldiers sang "Pack Up Your Troubles in Your Old Kit Bag" and "It's a Long Way to Tipperary," two World War I songs they'd learned just the day before, when I'd stayed out of school. Annie Sanderson came out wearing a top hat and a cape and did magic tricks. Barbara Andrews practically put the entire audience to sleep with the long poem she recited. Too bad Annie couldn't make Barbara disappear.

Paul Yamaguchi didn't get as much applause as I thought he would when he played "Rose of Washington Square," on his saxophone. It was his mother's favorite American melody and he put a lot of jazzy feeling into it. When it ended, from the wings backstage where those of us with "specialties" we were waiting to go on, I thought I heard a woman's voice shout something. I couldn't hear what it was, but the tone of voice sounded mean, so I could imagine it must have been more anti-Japanese name-calling.

Then, at last, it was Emi's and my turn to do our number. I was in my red velvet dress again and she was in a similar green one. We could see our moms sitting together in the front row.

Mrs. Rivington gave us a big introduction. "There are two girls in my class this year who have inspired me since I met them," she announced, "since they're both bright, vibrant, talented, and the very best of loyal friends. Their names are Ruby Rafferty and Emiko Fujiwara, so of course they've always been nicknamed 'Ruby and Emerald.' Ladies and Gentlemen, may I present The Gemstone Girls!"

There wasn't as much applause for us as I had thought, had hoped, there would be.

"Best friends?" I heard a lady at the far end of the front row screech as we took our places center stage.

"But one's a Jap!" exclaimed a man from the back of the room. His voice carried, loudly.

"Don't *start* that," commanded a shaky but familiar voice. It was my mother's.

They started regardless. The man called out, "Go back to Japan!"

Emi shot me a scared look. Scared of those two people in the audience, that is, not of performing. She'd never been afraid to perform in her life.

I shook my head slightly to show her that we should just ignore them. Miss Padegat struck up the piano, and we began to sing:

"Shine little glow worm, glimmer, glimmer …"

"Glimmer away from here!" yelled the man from the back.

"Shine little glow worm, glimmer, glimmer," we continued uncertainly.

"Lead us lest too far we wander,
Love's sweet voice is calling yonder…"

"Get out of this country!" shouted the woman. Her face got so red it was almost becoming purple. There was no sweet voice there.

Emi and I weren't sure what to do, but we knew the old saying among performers that no matter what happened, "the show must go on." We kept singing.

"Shine little glow worm, glimmer, glimmer,

Shine little glow worm, glimmer, glimmer,

Light the path below above,

And lead us on to love!"

"Lead you away, Jap girl!" a boy's voice called out. I recognized that one. It was Jessup Marz, at it again.

Emi and I exchanged a startled glance, then sang the next song:

"Be my little baby bumble-bee,

Buzz around, buzz around, keep a buzzin' 'round,

We'll be just as happy as can be,

You and me, you and me, you and me…"

"Happy, my foot! You're a traitor if you're singing with a Jap!" the same woman in the first row, several seats from where our mothers sat, called out, directing that particular nasty comment at me. She was clearly illuminated by the lights shining on us from the stage. Where had I seen her before? She had steel-gray hair that was too short, with bangs. Her mouth was turned down at the corners.

"Stop taunting these children!" Mrs. Rivington, who had stepped backstage, ran back out to roar at the audience. I never knew she could shout so loud. Our teacher remained on the side of the stage, arms folded, glaring. That shut the hecklers up.

Emi looked very embarrassed, as if she wanted to flee the stage, or maybe start to cry.

Over my dead body, I thought, will either one of us step down, no matter what some of these awful people were yelling at us. So I sang louder than ever, making a gesture with my right hand for her to raise her volume, too. Emi just stared at me. She looked frozen. Miss Padegat noticed and played a vamp on the piano, notes to give us time for Emi to get hold of herself. Thank God, I thought, for Miss Padegat.

Uncle Leo began to chant, "Gemstone Girls! Gemstone Girls!" He clapped with every syllable. Our mothers joined in. Other people in the audience started to pick up the chant, students, parents, friends, and all those people who still had the sense not to give in to indecency. They clapped along. It made me smile, though Emi still looked like she'd been punched in the stomach.

"Honey, keep a-buzzin', please," I found my voice and sang my solo as confidently as I could under the circumstances. I wanted to throw something at the people in the audience who had made those horrible comments, but instead I smiled as if the whole room loved me and tried to appear as calm as I could, even though I was boiling mad.

164

And I kept singing, loud and strong, since I knew if I didn't blow up or start to cry, Emi probably wouldn't either.

She didn't.

She was a beat behind, but Emi still sang her solo line, too. "I've got a dozen cousin bees…"

Together we went on,

"But I want you to be
My baby
Bumble bee!"

As we got to the end of the song, it came to me. I finally recognized the nervy lady who had called me a traitor. She was the one I'd seen the day I got the medicine for baby Hanae at Palmer's Drug Store. The mean one who had urged the druggist not to fill the prescription for anybody named Fujiwara.

Mrs. Stenzel. That was her name. Mr. Palmer had said it was as German a name as there could be, too. Well, I couldn't stand her on that first meeting on Pearl Harbor Day, and wished there was a handy bucket of water I could pour over her head now, but already had a thought of how to get spectacularly even.

When Emi and I finished the number, we sounded almost as confident and strong as we had during our rehearsals. I guess a lot of people in the audience were on our side after all, because we finished with a lot more applause than we'd started with.

"They should ship you Japs outta here," Mrs. Stenzel yelled when the applause died down.

"And take all of you *Germans* along, too, *Mrs. Stenzel*," I smiled sweetly, projecting so that my voice carried clearly to the rear of the auditorium. *Everybody* heard me. Take *that!*

The horrid woman let out a gasp, then shrieked, "How did that traitor girl know my last *name?"*

A lot of people laughed at that, including Mr. Winbury, who tried to stop himself but couldn't. He was standing over by the piano. "I'm glad she did. We are going to have to ask you to leave, *Frau* Stenzel," he ordered her. "You too, sir," he said to the man in the back. "And you, Jessup, once again, have misbehaved, so go home. We have no place here for anyone taunting our students."

"You can't call me *Frau!*" Mrs. Stenzel shrieked as he escorted her out the door. "I was born in Seattle!"

"So was Emiko," I shouted out. More laughter. People were laughing with me, not at me, so I didn't mind.

Mr. Winbury said, "Goodbye, *Frau* Stenzel! Be sure to take Jessup and this other rude man with you!" All three and their mean mouths were removed from the auditorium immediately. Mr. Winbury made a kicking motion with his leg as they left, creating a lot of laughter.

What I had just said may have gotten Mrs. Stenzel's goat, and rightly so, but it also upset poor Vera Manteffel. She was backstage and, as Emi and I walked off, looked ready to cry. "You want – us – Germans - leave?"

"No! Not you," I assured her. "Just that mean old gargoyle who was sitting out there," I said pointing. "She hates everyone Japanese. Remind me to tell you the whole story of what she said on Pearl Harbor Day about Emi's little sister's medicine later. Now it's your turn, so go out there and do a great job of singing!"

Vera didn't look like she fully understood me. I'd used too many English words, too quickly, and she usually only got about a third of what anyone said even when we talked extra slowly to her. "Go?" she repeated, as if I were in favor of sending her away.

"No, no, it's okay. I meant, go *sing!*" I specified, smiling in a way I hoped she'd see as encouraging. Poor kid, she was having such a hard time understanding English.

True to her promise, Miss Padegat had put the song lyrics to "White Cliffs of Dover" out on a music stand for Vera. Our new friend bravely went out front, as Mrs. Rivington introduced her as a little refugee from Hitler who was still learning our language.

167

"Ladies and gentlemen, this little European girl has courage in abundance. She's only just learned this hit song, and she's going to sing it to us in English. May I present to you the one, the only, the fabulous *Vera Manteffel!*"

Vera went out front and sang her song about the bluebirds and the peace the British were longing for beautifully. She once said *"weiss"* cliffs for "white" cliffs, but nobody noticed. She got a ton of applause at the end and couldn't stop beaming. Backstage, Emi, Paul, Sylvia, Christopher and I all took turns hugging her or patting her on the back. Daisy half-hugged her, too, that is with her free unbroken arm that wasn't in a sling.

"The way that kid can sing," Mrs. Rivington said to Emi and me backstage, "you should recruit her to join you onstage next time as your third Gemstone Girl. Where the English language is concerned, Vera may be a diamond in the rough. But a diamond in the rough is still a diamond. And diamonds are gemstones."

There were a few more numbers after Vera's that seemed to go on endlessly. After looking forward to this night and participating in this show for so long, I found I only wanted to get away from there. I was also afraid I might be in trouble for telling Mrs. Stenzel off. Mr. Winbury may not have minded. He was on the side of what was right. But my mother probably didn't like what I'd said, and Miss Bryce was in the audience, too. She'd probably say I had bad manners, at least, for what I'd done, and might even tell me off.

Finally the whole class was brought back on the stage to sing "God Bless America." I liked the idea of God blessing America but wished Miss Padegat would play the song a lot faster. I was looking forward to the moment when I could leave the building.

Punch and cookies were being served afterward but I said to Emi, "Want to just go?"

"As fast as possible," she replied. She didn't even want to leave the backstage area. "I don't want to go out there and be around all those people after what happened during our song. I've never wanted to be as invisible as I wish I could've been tonight! Would you go find our mothers, then come back here to get me so we can get away?"

"Of course, Emi." I was shocked at how clouded with misery her normally mischievous eyes looked. Emi had never been prone to embarrassment before this, I thought, as I dashed away to find our moms. It made me glad all over again to have said something to upset the Stenzel witch even if I might get in trouble over it. How could anybody be so awful? *How?*

Miss Bryce stopped me in the auditorium as I was about to find my mother and Emi's. Oh, here it comes, I thought. I'm in major trouble now!

But it turned out that I wasn't. "Not bad singing, Ruby! But my niece Millie in Portland could've sung it better," was all she said. She gave me a wink and a nod, and then clomped away.

Mom and Mrs. Fujiwara went with me to collect Emi from backstage. We made our escape through the nearest door. I wasn't in trouble. Both mothers were angry at the outbursts made by the rude adults and Jessup. "It's bad enough," my mother fumed as we strode home along the cold streets, "hideous, even, when children make fun of other children, but when grown men and women behave like that, and toward two little eleven-year-olds, I'm just flabbergasted!"

"The Stenzel dame is Jessup Marz's grandmother," said Emi. "I know because I saw her come to the school to pick him up one of the times when he got expelled."

"He has been expelled more than once?" Emi's mother asked. Her daughter nodded.

"Once a month, practically," I told them.

"Look at the grandmother he has and the example she sets," said Mom. "No wonder the boy is such a bad apple."

"I do not like to complain," Emi's mother said to mine, "but people are making things worse and worse for us. I was called names on our street while walking the dog. I am starting to hate to leave the house. The whole idea of my daughter being yelled at like that tonight..." her voice trailed off, not finishing the thought.

Molly Kimura was back at the Fujiwara house, listening to *Baby Snooks* on the radio while also keeping an eye on little Hanae, who was asleep in her cradle in the living room. I was so happy to get there for our sleepover and to be safely inside the soft blue-and-green sleekness of the Fujiwara house. Molly was staying the night, too. We all managed to fit into Emi's double bed and, with her bedside radio softly playing music, talked for a long time before falling asleep.

"What a terrible night this turned out to be," Emi sighed to her cousin, once the light was out and her mother was no longer in earshot. She explained everything that had happened.

"Tomorrow should be a fun day at school, at least," I said, trying to change the subject, "with the class Christmas party."

"I wish I never had to go back there," Emi sighed. "Ever! Not even tomorrow. Maybe I'll fake sick."

"You've never faked sick in your life," I reminded her.

"There's a first time for everything," said Molly.

Chapter Twelve: It's Out of Our Hands

Mrs. Rivington hung a new sign on the wall the next morning, a quote. It was:

"Fortune favors the bold."

"Like it? I'm putting this up here in honor of every last one of you for the great job you did last night at the talent show," she told us proudly. "But I especially want to single out Paul, Emi and Ruby." Emi had changed her mind about faking sick and was there beside me, as always, at school, not willing to miss the party or give Jessup the satisfaction of seeing her stay home.

I had been looking down at the top of my wooden desk, where several students from years past had etched their initials. I looked up now.

"The way the three of you kept right on performing last night while so much ugliness was being thrown in your direction was a sight to behold. Bravo!" Mrs. Rivington stood there and applauded us.

Then the whole class did, too. Emi and I even burst up and out of our seats to take a little bow. That was like something we used to do before this whole war thing started. Paul didn't, but for the first time since Pearl Harbor, he looked pleased.

Well, I should say that *almost* the whole class applauded. One student hung back, I noticed. It was Barbara. Who else?

"But I think we should discuss the current situation a little further, class," our teacher went on. "I realize there's a deluge of hostility being expressed against the Japanese children."

"And other Orientals too," Daisy Matapang put in. "I have the sling to prove it."

"We're at war with Germany and Italy too, but do you see half as much meanness going on towards the Germans and Italians?" Paul Yamaguchi asked hotly. "Not that I want to see that happen to them, either. I don't, not at all, but it's just the whole idea that we're at war with them, *too!* That lady last night who was yelling things at me, then at Emi and Ruby, she's from a German background, and she's got some nerve."

"Yes, Paul's right! If we're supposed to represent the enemy, then so does she," Marcie Hasegawa agreed. Boy, did she ever look mad!

"I heard that particular ill-mannered woman does have a German last name but is an American," said Mrs. Rivington, "born here, the same as most of us."

"There's even a new song about the Japanese," Sylvia said, "a horrible one, called 'You're a Sap Mr. Jap!'"

"And cartoons in the newspapers that draw us as buck-toothed slanty-eyed idiots," added Paul.

I was never so glad that my father had already left the newspaper as I was at that moment. Not that he had anything to do with the cartoons. He didn't. Still, I'd seen some of those drawings, and they were truly horrible.

"Propaganda," Mrs. Rivington explained. "Messages designed to unite us against the common enemy of the Japanese in Japan. Unfortunately it's terribly upsetting to those of us here who know the difference between the Japanese armed forces and our own Japanese American people, like those of you here in my class."

"We're not being treated like we were born here anymore," said Emi angrily. "That's the whole problem."

"I think that's because when people take one look at us, they can see we're Japanese. We can't pass for anything else," another Japanese girl, Mariko Morita, said bitterly.

I put up my hand and Mrs. Rivington said, "Yes, Ruby?"

"I think people are going crazy on the Japanese here in Seattle because, though we're at war with Germany and Italy too, the Japanese forces were the ones who got to Hawaii and attacked us *first*," I said. "Now the wrong people on the wrong continent are being blamed."

"That's it exactly," Marcie agreed.

Mrs. Rivington nodded. "Good assessment of it, Ruby. It's a terrible situation. I want every last one of you to know all the way through to your hearts that none of you children here had anything to do with that attack there. If anyone tries to convince you otherwise, or if they insult you or call you names, you need to know you're not responsible for their ill-bred behavior. They are."

"Know what someone's been calling my dad?" Christopher Callavari asked. "My father's family came from Italy. The rest of my family is Irish, but our last name's Italian. Well, we have a neighbor, an old codger who has always liked us before this, who's started calling my father 'Mussolini. My father doesn't even *like* Mussolini, let alone what he stands for."

"I was beaten up twice already, so I started telling people I'm Chinese," said Tatsuo Gima, "just so they would leave me alone."

"Twice? Oh, Tatsuo," said Mrs. Rivington, shaking her head.

"It's a horrible thing to say, because it's a lie," Tatsuo admitted, looking downward. "If my father ever finds out, he'll be so ashamed of me. But..."

"I agree it's not good to lie," our teacher said kindly, "but it's not good to get beaten up either. Especially when you've done nothing wrong and don't deserve it."

"People think we're not loyal Americans," complained Violet Shimono, "just because we're Japanese. Well my father was born here, my mother was born here, and I was born here. Why wouldn't I be loyal to my own country – *this* one?"

"I wish things could go back to the way they were before Pearl Harbor," spoke up shy Sachiko Ito, who rarely ever raised her hand to say anything. "I'm *so tired* of being called names."

"Everywhere I go, me too," said Paul Yamaguchi. *"Everywhere."*

Mrs. Rivington winced. "The people who are doing that are behaving like barbarians."

"I was supposed to go on Christmas vacation with Ruby. Her parents wound up cancelling our trip because of the war, but if they hadn't, I wasn't going to be allowed to go," complained Emi, "because the government doesn't want us 'Japs' to ride anywhere. We can't go on the trains. They won't allow us on airplanes or buses, either. I hate this!"

"I would hate it too," said Mrs. Rivington emphatically. "With my whole heart."

"My parents said after the show last night that what's happening is a shame," Sylvia Lindstrom said. "Seattle's such a nice city. Folks here always got along pretty well before this, no matter where our families came from originally."

"Keep in mind," Mrs. Rivington pointed out, "that even though a few people in the audience were very, very rude last night, the majority of them weren't. Everyone else enjoyed the show and loved your performances."

"I loved," I spoke up, "how Vera's uncle got so many of the good people in the audience to clap for us and cheer us on."

"Yes, your family is great," Momoko smiled at Vera, who looked pleased.

"The trick," Mrs. Rivington said warmly, "is to try to do whatever we can, in bad circumstances, to make the situation better rather than worse."

"But it's out of our hands," said a red-haired boy named Douglas Medford. "Like Emi not being able to ride the train with Ruby because there's a war regulation against letting the Japanese travel. How do we make *that* better?"

"That, we can't help right now," said our teacher with a sad shake of her head. "It's a wartime regulation. It's terrible, yet it's happening."

"There doesn't even seem to be any way around it," I said. "As soon as I heard about that, I wanted to try to fight it, and get Emi permission to go with me, as planned. But there isn't even anyone I could ask to let her be the exception to such an awful rule. Now we're not going anyway, but still."

"It's going to be difficult for quite awhile, I expect," explained our teacher, "since you were lucky enough to grow up during peacetime, and are used to being free to do whatever you wanted. It looks like wartime, especially this time around, is going to be very different, with all kinds of restrictions. But things can change. Any time you come across a chance to make a bad situation better, please, take it. Meanwhile, I want every last one of you to keep holding your heads up high and not let anyone else's attitude defeat you. We can also do as Ruby did last night: stand up and say something when someone else is being vicious to one of our Japanese friends here in Seattle who *did not* lead any attacks on Hawaiian harbors."

And to think I'd been afraid I'd get in trouble for the way I let the Stenzel woman have it! Instead I was being praised for doing the right thing.

Mrs. Rivington laughed a tiny bit. "You know, there was a time years back when teachers were supposed to tell you that, as children, your purpose was to be 'seen and not heard,' to be quiet and stay in the background. But today, I'm saying the opposite. Be proud of who you are, and don't ever be afraid to speak out and help friends, especially if they need you to stand up and be one."

"But the Japanese *attacked* us," Barbara Andrews made the mistake of saying under her breath, or thinking she had, at just that moment. It came out louder than she realized.

"No one *here* attacked you, Barbara," I said, rolling my eyes at how clueless she was. "Can't you tell the difference between your own Japanese schoolmates and the

Japanese Navy? I'm really getting sick and tired of the things you've been saying about the Japanese."

"Me too," said Douglas.

"Me three," said Sylvia in a scared tone, since she used to be Barbara's best friend.

"Me four," exclaimed Mrs. Rivington in her toughest no-nonsense voice. "Barbara, you need to develop a better and smarter attitude about the way things really are. You may want to find enemies to blame for Pearl Harbor among your classmates, but to do so is ridiculous! My own son was attacked by the Japanese in Hawaii, and I don't hate these Japanese children here in my class in Seattle, so why should you? The real enemies are in the Japanese government and military, living under the red and white sun flag of Japan, far across the sea."

"Yeah," said Douglas. "They're not here."

"All of us here live under a different flag. The stars and stripes! Now back to the quote," Mrs. Rivington went on. It's a Roman proverb, written by someone who once lived in what is now modern-day Italy. Is it any less nice because of what's going on there these days with the Italian dictator Mussolini on the march?"

"No," several of us said in unison.

"Of course not," our teacher grinned. "Do you understand the point I'm trying to get across?"

"That we can't blame the Roman who wrote the quote back then for what's going on there now?" asked Emi with just a trace of her old bright smile back on her face. "Like you can't throw out the baby with the bathwater?"

"*Exactly!* And like the quote says, you need to have some guts to get anywhere, even through a song number in an audience with hecklers.*"*

I loved Mrs. Rivington for that lesson. The war had already caused too many rough patches and it was only a week and a half old. She was trying her best to smooth everything over for us.

The atmosphere became a lot more pleasant the following Tuesday. That was the last day of school before Christmas vacation, and our class had a Christmas party.

Most of us had brought in treats to share. My contribution was a big bag of butterscotch candies with enough for everyone to get at least three. There were cupcakes from Annie, cookies from Paul, sodas and chocolates, too.

Barbara Andrews, who was subdued after everything that had been said to her that morning, brought everyone a Tootsie Pop. She was trying to act a little bit nicer. Even though I normally loved Tootsie Pops, I really didn't feel right about taking one from *her*. She gave it to me anyway, and as soon as she went further down my row to give one to

Emi, who sat right behind me, I quickly put mine on Paul's desk. Emi followed suit, putting hers on Vera's.

"By the way," I said to Vera, "Emi and I were talking about it and we decided. Next time there's a class talent show, we'd love it if you could be the third Gemstone Girl." That took us awhile to explain. Vera was delighted when she finally figured out what we meant.

Mrs. Rivington had brought in a lot of treats, too, including a big vanilla frosted cake. She didn't stop there. Our teacher had also made up little bags of presents for every single one of us. Each of us got a brand new box of twelve colored pencils and a sketch pad. Everybody also received an apple, an orange, some taffy, hard candies and a candy cane.

"I couldn't resist," Mrs. Rivington confided to me in a whisper, giving me a squeeze, when I told her she was like our very own Christmas elf. "You children were all so wonderful the way you welcomed me back, and made cards for my boy, and I *truly* wanted to do something to cheer everybody up, especially the Japanese kids. They're really getting put through the wringer."

Emi, Vera, Daisy and I walked home from school together, in a better mood than usual after the nice party. It lasted until a beautifully dressed young woman in a royal blue coat with a wide fur collar that I'd never seen before passed us on the sidewalk, walking a Schnauzer puppy. She took one look at Emi and Daisy, then at Vera and me. She shook her head, walked past us, but suddenly turned back. She stopped next to me and asked, "Could I maybe have a word with you, hon?"

At first I thought maybe she was new to our neighborhood and needed directions, so of course I replied, "Sure." I was even about to ask where she wanted to go when the lady in blue gestured that we walk a few steps away from the others. Once she felt we were safely out of their earshot, she lowered her voice to a sickeningly sweet but hushed tone and addressed me. "Don't you know," she asked me softly, gesturing to Emi and Daisy, "that *all* those people want to do is destroy us, and the country we love?"

Daisy, once again, had been mistaken for Japanese, but the stranger had accurately figured out Emi's background.

"You must be a terribly misguided child, considering those you're with. Surely," she went on in her whisper, "a girl like you doesn't belong with *them?*" She made the last word sound like it was some kind of a curse.

Was I ever furious! I wanted to tell her off. I wanted to say she didn't know what she was talking about, that friends are friends, and that kids weren't responsible for the actions of the Japanese armed forces. I wanted to answer her whispers with a roar and shout this at the top of my lungs. The only thing that stopped me was that we'd just come from enjoying our school celebration and I didn't want Emi and Daisy to realize they were being looked down upon *again*. Enough people made them feel terrible already without me adding to it.

So I merely kept my own voice as low as I could and, with a blazing mad look in my eyes, replied, "Why don't you just mind your own damn business and find something better to do than bother me?" Before she had a chance to respond, I turned on my heel and caught up with the others. That woman had been wearing such a pretty outfit, but there was so much ugliness inside of her!

Emi asked me what she'd wanted. I said it wasn't anything, the lady was just lost, but I couldn't really face her when I said it. Emi could see that something had gone wrong. She let out a little cry, and gritted her teeth. "Another one, was it? Ruby, I can't take much more! I'm going to have to think of something I can do about all this."

That night, wanting to do something that would feel normal, I found an old issue of *Photoplay* magazine that had quite a few pictures of my favorite star, Carole Lombard, in it. I had hair ribbons at the ready and some bobby pins, too. Maybe I wasn't going to California on the train the next day, but I wanted a movie star hairdo. Carole Lombard wore her hair parted on the side, pinned in the front, wavy and billowy in the back. I undid my pigtails and kept trying to do mine a similar way but without success.

I had bangs, and I was tired of them. They were too short to look good when I tried to brush them aside after making a side part. I re-did them back the way they'd been, then tried to bobby-pin my hair up on either side, like Lombard's. At least my hair was naturally wavy so I got the billowy part in the back down pat without trying, but the rest was hardly a success.

I was just thinking I'd have to grow my bangs out for awhile, then try again in a few months, when the doorbell rang. I could hear Mom cross the living room, where she had been listening to *The Kate Smith Hour* on the radio, to answer the door.

"Ruby," she called up the stairs, "come on down, will you?"

I wondered who it could be, since as far as I knew we hadn't been expecting anyone.

It was Mrs. Rosi Manteffel and Vera. Both of them couldn't stop smiling.

"What's got you both looking so happy?" I asked. Then I thought I knew the answer. "Did you hear from your cousin Mitzi?"

"How kind of you to ask. Unfortunately that miracle hasn't happened yet," Mrs. Manteffel said.

Mom said, "Rosi was just delivering some goodies I ordered from the Manteffels store, Ruby. You'll find out about them soon."

"How soon?"

"Oh, I don't know. Maybe on Christmas Day," said Mom with a mysterious wink.

"Really?" Now I was wearing a smile, too. So *that* had been what our mothers were talking about yesterday!

"Vera, can you, at least, give me a hint, just one little one, about whatever it is they're not telling me?" I asked, but of course Vera didn't understand the word "hint." She shrugged, puzzled, and unable to answer my question.

It didn't matter. Mom brought out a plate of cookies and made tea for herself and Rosi. She poured glasses of milk and spooned in chocolate Ovaltine for Vera and me. "Cookies and milk," I said to Vera, "are good in any language." I think she understood me because she smiled. "To the new Gemstone Girl!" We clinked glasses as if we were making a toast.

Chapter Thirteen: A Wartime Christmas

The next day it was Christmas Eve.

It was strange to be shopping for a Christmas tree without my father, who always drove us to a stand on Denny Way, and then would tie the tree onto the car roof for the short ride home. Mom explained, the next morning, we would be going to a closer tree seller's stall this year, and would have to get a tree that was smaller than usual. There was only one way we were going to be able to get our tree home and that was by carrying it ourselves.

"A smaller tree is fine," I said, and it was, but I loved our old family tradition of always having a great *big* tree set up in the living room. Mom's not having a driver's license had never been a problem before Dad enlisted, but it was better not to complain. Besides, I had glanced at the newspaper that morning. There were battles being fought in Europe and Asia. I was old enough to realize that my not having a certain type of Christmas tree was not the worst thing going on in the world. We'd make do.

The little one we found wasn't as tall as I was, but it was light, even with a wooden base attached to the bottom. The tree seller wrapped paper around it. Mom held the front, I held the back, and we managed to get it home.

"Why don't you ask Emi to come over," she suggested, once the tiny tree was trying its best to stand proudly in a corner of the living room. It looked so small and bare. "We can make some popcorn. You can eat some and string the rest into a garland for the tree, then decorate it."

It seemed as good an idea as any, so I ran next door and brought Emi back. By then my mother had already put the oil on the stove to heat for the popcorn. She left the room when the telephone rang. I could hear her side of the conversation. It was Madge Barclay, inviting Mom and me to their house for a Christmas Eve party that night.

Emi looked like she had been crying, I realized as she sat across from me at the kitchen table. "Hey, what's wrong?" I asked her.

"There's still no word about my father," Emi explained glumly with her chin on her hands. "My mother is so upset. She thinks maybe we don't hear from him because he's dead. Not just arrested, *dead*. I'm getting even more scared than I've been already. What if she's right?"

It was hard to figure out what to say. I was secretly afraid something terrible had happened to Emi's father, too, but I didn't want to say so or Emi might feel worse. "Just about every kid in our class who's Japanese has a father missing, or a grandfather," I finally said. "They can't *all* be dead. You're bound to hear something soon. Maybe he'll be home by Shogatsu." Shogatsu was the Japanese name for the New Year's holiday. The Fujiwaras always had a big party. They put up red decorations, since red was considered the color of good fortune. There were even red treats to eat, including red-colored rice balls and lobster. I looked forward to Shogatsu every year.

"We won't be having our Shogatsu party. Mama already said," Emi told me.

Mom heard what we were talking about. "Well, Emerald and Ruby, we've all been invited to the Manteffels for New Year's," she said brightly, "so there will still be a party. In the meantime, little ladies, we have a tree to decorate. You two need to start stringing the popcorn."

We didn't stop there. We made lots of Christmas crafts that day, paper chains for the tree, and paper candy canes, too. We found last year's tinsel, lights and ornaments, and were able to put some, if not all, of those up, too, since this tree was too small for the whole works to fit. Just the same, it turned out to be a really pretty tree once we turned on the colored lights. Later Emi and I sang carols as we made Christmas cookies. She brought some home to her mother. It had been such a nice, peaceful day that I was almost able to forget about the war mess.

That feeling of calm lasted until the evening. Emi went home right before Colonel Barclay stopped by to pick Mom and me up. They lived in a pretty white house in the Rainier Beach neighborhood, clear on the other side of Seattle. Inside they had set up a gorgeous Christmas tree with blue lights, and it almost touched the high living room ceiling. Garlands of evergreen branches with blue and silver balls hanging from them trimmed the fireplace mantle. Pretty.

Some of the other guests didn't even seem to notice how nice the decorations looked. They were too busy carrying on about the Japanese.

"I heard people are seriously calling for all of the west coast Japanese to be rounded up and sent far away, where they can't do any more harm," a man I recognized as one of the Barclays' neighbors, who was about forty years old, said happily as we ate shrimp cocktail at Madge's beautifully set table. "Locked up, even."

"All of them?" a woman asked.

"Every last one," the man said forcefully. His chilling tone made my stomach begin to ache. So did his words.

"Impossible," declared a younger man that I recognized. He was an older reporter Dad used to be friends with at the newspaper, one who hadn't enlisted yet. Colonel Barclay, after all, was the former editor, so the party guests were a mix of reporters and men from the National Guard and their wives and children. Some of the guardsmen were even in uniform.

"Oh, it's very possible," countered the neighbor.

"Just how many Japs are there on the west coast? And where could we put them?" another woman asked.

"Thousands and thousands. Preferably we could ship them all right back to Japan," the neighbor said, answering both questions. "Failing that, who knows? We have thousands here, and they're probably all in touch with the Emperor. We'd be well rid of them, and let's face it, we never should have let them come here in the first place. Look what they did to Hawaii!"

I couldn't keep silent. "It was the Japanese military that attacked Hawaii, not the Japanese people living here in Seattle," I spoke up, sounding a lot like Mrs. Rivington. Better to sound like her than either one of the Barclays.

The room fell silent. Colonel Barclay's mouth fell open. He looked as though he thought I'd just gone completely crazy.

To the others he cleared his throat and explained, "Ah, don't mind little Ruby, here. She goes to school with quite a few Japanese children."

"She's in the same school with *them?*" The neighbor all but exploded, as though this was something terrible. "Poor little girl!"

"Ruby, dear," Madge suggested mildly, "don't you think you might be a lot happier going to *another* school, where you can meet your *own* kind of children?"

Why were the Barclays always carrying on about me attending some other school?

"She may not have to," said an older man in a National Guard uniform before I could answer Madge with a great, big, loud, "No!" "I've heard General De Witt of the Western Defense Command is in favor of sending the Japs away, and if that happens, Ruby will be with her own kind soon enough. There won't be any other kind left." Several people at the party laughed. One said, "Good, tell them *sayonara!*" The Japanese word for "goodbye."

My mother didn't let them get away with it. She took a deep breath and spoke up. "Even the children in my daughter's class? Do all of you really believe that if a bunch of Seattle *elementary* school children are sent away it will somehow protect America from another Pearl Harbor?"

That caused the whole room to go silent.

The neighbor let out a guffaw. "Heck, yes!" He slapped his leg as he laughed, and a few of the others joined in. I gave him the dirtiest look I could work up.

"Well," Colonel Barclay spoke up, "it's their parents who are the real problem, Ruby. There's a genuine threat of sabotage from these Japanese."

"Then how come there haven't been any cases if it already?" I shot right back.

Mom grinned at that. "She's got you there," she said to the Colonel.

"She's good at getting me, this kid is," the Colonel said, but he winked at me as he said it.

I had been happy to go to this party since Madge was a great cook, but after that conversation, I found it hard to eat. My stomach muscles seemed to have been tied into knots. Could what they were saying actually happen?

* * * * *

I woke up later than usual the next day, even though it was Christmas morning. Mom came into my room, when she heard me stirring, to wish me a Merry Christmas. I wished her one back. She said she was surprised I hadn't been up at the crack of dawn, all set to go to the earliest possible church service, the better to get home and open my presents, like last year and every year before.

"It just doesn't seem like it's Christmas," I explained, "not with Pearl Harbor, Dad in the service, and everything else."

"But it still is," Mom said. "It's the day when people all over the world celebrate the birth of Jesus, so 'tis the season to be jolly. There's no need to look so glum. Make an effort to keep your chin up! Get dressed and let's go to church."

"Okay," I agreed, without much enthusiasm. We should have been waking up in Hollywood, California this morning, which was part of the "everything else" that made this Christmas not seem so merry.

"You're really growing up on me," Mom smiled as we left the house to walk to our church a few minutes later. "Time was when all you could think about at this time of year was Christmas. You could hardly wait, when you were little, to see what Santa left for you under the tree. I remember when you were four years old, awake in your bed on Christmas Eve, and called out to your father and me, 'Santa's here! He's here! I hear a reindeer on the roof!'"

I smiled at that. "I said that?"

"You sure did! Your father and I thought it was hilarious."

"Ha, good old Santa."

Mom and I attended the next scheduled service at our church. There were four candles lit and shining on the Advent wreath this week, just like always. It was nice to know that the same old traditions continued there, and wouldn't be changing, especially this year, when everything else had. I prayed for more than presents this year: that the rumors I'd heard last night at the Barclays' house wouldn't happen, that Daddy would come home soon, that the Manteffels would locate Mitzi and her mother and father, and that the world could return to peacetime status. So many countries were fighting with so many others at this point that I knew this was a pretty tall order.

I hadn't really expected Mom to get me presents because the cancelled trip to Hollywood would have been the biggest gift of the year, but she surprised me. Back at the house, as soon as Mom put the cinnamon rolls in the oven for a special Christmas breakfast, she brought me over to see what was waiting for me under the tree. There were several beautifully wrapped gifts.

Mom had bought me a pretty new flowered blouse, a blue velvet winter dress with a white lace collar and cuffs, a pink flannel nightgown, and three new Nancy Drew mystery books. Three! She gave me a new set of watercolor paints, too. I also opened a fluffy white sweater knitted by Madge Barclay and a five-dollar bill in a card from the Colonel. A slender box wrapped in silvery paper contained a new blue fountain pen. It had come in the mail from Mom's sister Kate in New York City who I still hadn't met because she lived so far away. Aunt Kate always sent me a nice present.

Just when I thought everything had been opened, I was given a tiny box wrapped in red shiny paper with a beautiful darker red satin bow on top.

"I've saved the best for last. Open it," Mom urged me, smiling.

Underneath the wrapping paper, the white box was printed with the words *Manteffel's Jewelry Store* in fancy gold letters. It was for me. Wow! I'd never gotten a gift from Manteffel's before! I opened it, and could hardly believe my eyes when I saw what was inside. The present was a tiny oval ruby pendant, trimmed with small diamonds, on a golden chain.

"A ruby," I said happily. "It's a real genuine ruby!" It was an actual jewel! A gemstone! I was born in July, so ruby was my birthstone as well as my name. I put it right on.

"That's the surprise Rosi and Vera Manteffel were delivering to the house the other night, the one I've been planning with Rosi. Your father," Mom told me, getting misty-eyed, "right before he left to join up, said he wanted me to order this for you. Normally we'd have waited until you turned sweet sixteen to give you such a grown-up gift, but – well, he wanted you to have a necklace as nice as this one right now." Mom didn't have to explain any more, but I could figure out the rest of what she meant. Daddy was afraid of not letting me get the ruby now, just in case something were to happen to him on the battlefield, he didn't come home, and he never had the chance to give me this fine present.

"I love it," I said, starting to cry. "I can't wait to write him and tell him how much!"

Later that day Daddy surprised us by calling from the pay phone at Fort Lewis. I was able to tell him how much I loved the ruby, and him, and how very much I missed him, on the phone instead. He said his training was going well, but as one of the "older men" in the unit at the "advanced" age of thirty-two, it wasn't that easy.

"I think it's good that you're sticking with it anyway," I told him. "Keep at it! I still want you to capture some Nazis. A whole platoon of them!" Then at Dad's insistence, I gave the phone to Mom, who talked to him until he ran out of change and the pay phone cut off the call.

"He said," she told me, laughing, "those Nazis better take cover and watch out, because he's planning to zap plenty of them when he gets there--on his daughter's orders."

It turned out to be a really special Christmas after all.

Later that week, things began to look up, at least a little bit. It said in the paper that in the other Washington, the one in D.C., Winston Churchill, Prime Minister of England, was spending the holiday with President Roosevelt and Eleanor at the White House. He'd secretly sailed on a ship for ten days to get there, which was incredibly dangerous, since the waters of the Atlantic were full of German submarines. Any of them might have torpedoed his boat, had the Nazis known who was on it, but they didn't, and Churchill made it.

"The man has got to have guts galore to set sail under those circumstances," I said admiringly.

"This can only be a good development," Mom observed. "Roosevelt and Churchill are surely not just celebrating Christmas. They're planning the strategy to win the war."

On New Year's Eve morning there was even, finally, some positive war news coming from Asia: the Japanese were having a hard time in Manila. New U.S. warplanes had arrived to fight them. Aha, I thought, look out, Pacific - *the Yanks have come!* This was the beginning of rousting the Japanese out.

"Could Dad's prediction that the war would be over within a year come true?" I asked the adults at the Manteffel's New Year's Eve dinner that night.

"I'm not sure it's likely, Ruby. But here's hoping," Uncle Leo said, raising his glass of champagne.

I toasted him back with my Coca-Cola bottle. "Yes! Here's hoping."

Chapter Fourteen: Don't Lose Heart

A few days later, when Mom and I came home from the grocery store, lugging bags, we were greeted by the last sight I ever expected to see happening right in front of our house and Emi's: Vera's Uncle Leo was teaching Emi's mother how to drive.

Or maybe I should say he was *trying* to teach her. She was sitting in the driver's seat of her imprisoned husband's car, with Uncle Leo beside her, and it looked like she was wailing. The last thing Noriko had ever wanted to do was operate a car. She always said a car was "like a beast with wheels."

Emi was outside, with her Scottie dog Buddy on a leash, watching with concern while shaking her head. The baby was inside the house with her cousin Molly. Her mother, she said, had no desire to steer "the beast" away from the curb.

That morning they had finally found out where Emi's father was. The mystery was solved. He'd been taken to a prison in, of all places, Wyoming. His jailers finally let him send his family a letter.

Uncle Leo and Aunt Manya had decided to step in and try to assist Emi's mother, just as Mom and I kept trying to do. Since she didn't know how to drive, Leo thought the first thing he should do was teach her so she'd have the ability to get around better than she could at the moment, without her husband, and with nothing but public transportation to rely on. Unfortunately, she was too fearful of driving a car for his good idea to work out well.

He gave up, asked Emi's mother to turn off the ignition, and left the car to speak to my mother. "Mary, you don't know how to drive either, and with your husband away, you should learn, the same as Noriko. Nori's terrified. She might not be if you were to get behind the wheel first for a lesson. What do you say?"

"Excellent idea," is what Mom said, surprising me. "I'll just bring these bags inside the house, come back out and give it a whirl."

I talked to Emi on her front stairs. "I'm so glad you finally heard from your father! But I don't get it. Why did they send him to Wyoming?" I asked. "I thought he would be somewhere closer to home."

Emi shrugged. "If I knew, I could tell you, but I don't. The FBI or whoever is in charge of Papa's arrest probably doesn't want him anywhere near here," she said bitterly. "They've sent him so far away from the coast we can't even visit! That's the worst part. But he did write and ask us for clean shirts and a few other items, which we're going to send in a package this afternoon."

"At least now you know where he is, and that he's alive."

"Yes. My mother is so relieved. Me too."

"In one way, you're lucky, even though you probably won't think so," I said hesitantly. "So long as your father's in jail, even though it's not right, at least he won't be on the front lines of the war, where he might get shot, like mine could. Which doesn't mean I think yours belongs in jail," I added quickly.

Emi nodded. "I never thought of it like that, Ruby, but it's a good point."

Noriko looked relieved to give up the driver's seat and move to the back when my mother came outside and took her place. Uncle Leo resumed his lesson with a new pupil. Fortunately Mom wasn't afraid to learn. She looked thrilled.

When school started again, Emi began wearing dark sunglasses when she walked on the street, even on the cloudiest of Seattle winter days. I asked her why. She whispered it was to hide the shape of her eyes so that people wouldn't call her a "Slanty-Eyed Jap" any longer.

It was hard for me not to cry for her when she said that. I blinked my tears back—they would have made her feel worse—and simply commented that she probably wouldn't be allowed to keep those glasses on in the classroom. Emi just shrugged. "So I'll put them in my coat pocket when I hang it up, but I'm wearing them from now on when I'm on the street." I wanted to object to the idea of my best friend feeling like she needed to hide who she was, just to stop the abuse she kept on receiving, but the forceful note in her tone made me hold my tongue for one of the few times in my life. If wearing sunglasses made things easier for her, who was I to say she shouldn't have to do that? I wasn't the one who was being called names. Still, it hurt to see her wear them.

Barbara Andrews began walking with us again. I ignored her. Chester Yang, incredibly, tried to join us that first day back, too. He was now sporting a button that said I AM CHINESE so nobody would mistake him for Japanese.

He only attempted to walk with us that one time. There wasn't a single one of the rest of us First Avenue North kids who wanted him around after the things he and Jessup had done to us, not even Barbara.

"What do you want to be seen with us for, all of a sudden?" I asked him irritably, the second he tried it. "We're garbage to you, scum, aren't we? We're all Japs and Jap lovers, or so you used to say. Where's your blockhead of a buddy, Jessup Marz?"

"He doesn't go to our school any longer," Chester said glumly. "His parents have sent him to military school in the hopes it would straighten him out."

That was the first big surprise of 1942, and about the only one that would prove to be pleasant.

The next one wasn't. It was Proclamation 2537, and it had Emi's mother hysterical in my mother's kitchen after it was announced in the middle of January.

The proclamation declared that "enemy aliens" from Japan, Germany or Italy were now required to report any change of address, employment or name to the FBI.

"Relax," my mother tried to calm Noriko down, "you haven't moved, you don't have a new job, and you haven't changed your name. There's nothing for you to report, Nori."

"It does not matter," Noriko practically wailed. "It is next step toward trouble for us."

Mom and I exchanged a look, and I nodded slightly, agreeing with Nori. It wasn't good that the FBI kept watching the whole Japanese community so closely.

After Nori went home, my mother said that about all we could do for her and Emi right now was to try to make them feel better. "I think she's right, and it's about to get seriously worse on the Japanese," she told me. "They need friends now more than ever."

Three days later, something happened to make me forget about the proclamation, and, for that matter, just about everything else.

It was a Saturday morning. When I went outside to get the newspaper for Mom, I saw the headline. The horrible, terrible, most unexpected headline. It said, though it couldn't be, *CAROLE LOMBARD AND 21 OTHERS BELIEVED KILLED IN AIRLINE CRASH.*

Emi must have seen the paper at about the same time because I no sooner had it in the house than she came running over.

The awful article said that my favorite star, Carole, had gone to Indiana, her home state, to raise money for the war by selling war bonds. They worked just like savings bonds. If you bought one for $18.75, you could get $25.00 back, ten years later. My favorite star had done a splendid job selling them, too, raising over two million dollars in one day to help us fight.

Carole had been scheduled to return home to California on a train, but at the last minute decided it would be quicker to fly back on an airplane. It may have been faster, but not by much. The plane had to make several stops to refuel. After it took off from Las Vegas, on the last leg home, it had crashed into a nearby mountain. Every single person on the plane, including 15 army pilots and Carole Lombard's mother, were believed dead. Clark Gable's heart was broken. He had rushed to the area of the crash to see if there would be any good news of his wife, but it looked like none would come.

I was shocked. How and why could this have happened? Carole was so pretty and talented! She was funny and gutsy, too. She was everything I wished to be when I grew up. Why did she have to take that plane?

"Maybe they'll still be able to find her," I said hopefully, since the alternative was too horrible to think about, "alive. Maybe she made it. We should wait until they're sure." I didn't cry. I wasn't going to cry unless she really was gone. It was hard not to, though.

"Oh, Ruby," was all my mother could say.

By the next morning, they were sure. Everyone on board that plane was dead.

That's when I went back up to my room and cried into my pillow, wishing more than ever that the war had never happened let alone brought the need for stars to sell war bonds with it.

* * * * *

Christopher Callavari, who had never noticed me before, felt sorry for me after Carole Lombard died. The next morning at school he gave me a candy bar. That afternoon, when Mrs. Rivington announced she was putting me in charge of a class bake sale to raise war bond money like my hero had done, I gladly accepted the challenge, and picked Christopher as my second-in-command.

On the same day in early February that "Deep in the Heart of Texas" appeared on *Your Hit Parade*, which I was listening to at Emi's, she told me the latest bad news. Curfews had been put into effect, throughout the Pacific coast, for Japanese people *only*. They were now prohibited from leaving their houses between eight o'clock at night until six o'clock in the morning!

"It's only going to make my mother keep me home more than ever, even during the hours we're allowed to be out," she complained to me in a whisper. Her mother still wouldn't let her go with the rest of the kids to the movies like she used to. I felt bad because Vera and I were becoming inseparable every Saturday, going to the theater together, and Emi, due to her mother, was left out.

Mom felt Emi's mother was right to keep her home. "Imagine how you'd feel if Emi joined you and was beaten up or hurt by some nut like the Marz brat, or his horrible grandmother, who blame her for Hawaii. That theater you kids love so much is quite a hike from here and a lot could happen to Emi on the way. There's still too much hysteria out there."

"But Emi shouldn't have to stay inside all the time, like a prisoner," I complained. "You should talk to Noriko about it." Mom did. It did no good. Noriko continued to prevent Emi from going anywhere except school.

President Roosevelt instituted Year-Round Daylights Saving Time a few days after that. It was officially called "Pacific War Time." The clocks were put forward an hour. We had extra sunlight every day, which was lovely, yet other things became more and more bleak.

Dad wrote me, saying, "What do you get when you take the impossible and add the illogical? Boot camp!" He was almost done with the training and said he certainly wouldn't miss it. Dad added he was trying to get accepted into a "specialized training program next," but didn't say what kind.

The war was always with us, whether we would have loved to forget about it or not. Camouflage netting had been put over the Boeing plant, where warplanes were in production, to make sure no Japanese pilots who might fly overhead could see it from the air. Anti-aircraft guns were set up in the Seattle parks to shoot down Japanese planes, should they ever arrive. I was glad to be old enough to not want to go to the playground any longer because now it wasn't possible to ride the swings near those big guns anyway. Some days I felt so much more grown up than I ever had before, no longer concerned with things like swings.

Blue-star banners became the latest rage. They could be seen in homes all over town. If you had a family member in the military, you hung one up in your front window. I was proud we had a banner in ours, hung up in honor of Daddy's service. It had a blue star in the middle of a white rectangle on a red rectangle. Red, white and blue, our national colors. It looked pretty sharp in our window. I just hoped the day would never dawn when we would need to take it down and replace it with a gold-star banner. That's the one families displayed if their serviceman died in battle.

On Valentine's Day, the jaunty new song on the *Hit Parade* was "Remember Pearl Harbor." It was like a battle cry. Despite its upbeat melody, I just didn't like it. I even had a strange feeling that it was the first hint of something worse, about to come.

On February 19th, it turned out I was right. President Roosevelt signed another proclamation. This one was called Executive Order 9066.

It allowed for the Secretary of War, or any military commander, to create "military areas" within the country. They could then decree that "certain people" had to be "excluded" from those particular strategic zones.

Certain people. Japanese people?

asked Mom. She said yes, that in all probability, it was the Japanese who were going to be moved out, and soon. I knew it. Who else would the military move out? Would the Italians and the Germans have to go too?

"Would President Roosevelt really do this?" I asked.

"If he signed that executive order, then he already has, yes," said Mom, her blue eyes wide in shock. "And if you ask me, he's being ridiculous! I can hardly believe good old President Roosevelt would make a move as strange as this, against all the Japanese. He's the same man I used to think was fantastic when he said, during all the major money problems we had during The Great Depression, that 'the only thing we have to fear is fear itself.'"

I asked, "Think Seattle's going to be in the evacuation zone?"

"I certainly hope not," Mom replied, "though we're on the Pacific Coast, and since Japan is across the Pacific, we probably will be, yes. Pray!"

Mom and I were in the minority where this awful idea of a Japanese evacuation was concerned. Most Americans were in favor of the idea of moving them "somewhere inland," away from the coast. Even the American Legion, an organization for war veterans, was all for it. They praised the idea in the papers. I thought our whole country was going nuts.

Right after that we found out an evacuation was already about to happen just one week later at Terminal Island, near Los Angeles. The Japanese living there were told they had just a week before they'd be moved out! The next day the Japanese kids in my class were very upset and so were the rest of us, except for Barbara. She said right out loud she would feel safer when the "Jap spies" left.

Mariko Morita stuck her foot in the aisle and tripped her when she came back into the classroom after getting sent to Mr. Winbury's office by Mrs. Rivington for another talking-to, which nobody figured would help. Barbara fell flat on her face.

On March 2nd, we found out where the zones were. The western half of Washington, Oregon, California, and the southern portion of Arizona, had been declared as "military zones" by General DeWitt. All Japanese persons, and ones of Japanese descent, would have to be removed from those areas. Seattle, of course, was located in the western half of Washington. Every one of the nine Japanese students in my class, and their parents, were going to be sent away against their will.

Not the people of German ancestry, like Jessup Marz and the Stenzler witch. Not the ones with Italian nationalities in their backgrounds, like Christopher Callavari. Only the Japanese ones had to go.

Mrs. Rivington was beside herself at the thought, grabbing at her pearls. "You realize," she said, looking as though she were reaching for some decent reason why such a thing would be taking place, "that many sacrifices have to be made, by each and every one of us, in wartime. Maybe the one the Japanese population has to make is to temporarily leave. It's horrible! It can't be worse, actually. But, children, those who are asked to move out one day might very well be allowed to move back another. Please. *Don't lose heart."*

I knew she was trying to keep things upbeat, but it didn't ring true because she was blinking back tears as she tried to smile and say it. Besides, she didn't say they *would* move back. She said they *might be allowed.*

Sachiko Ito started to sob and had to leave the room. Tatsuo Gima, the boy who had told people the fib that he was Chinese so they wouldn't hassle him for being Japanese, ran out next, probably so we wouldn't see him crying, either. Mrs. Rivington let them go, putting her head in her hands on her desk for a moment before taking hold of herself. I thought she was ready to cry, too. Emi, in the desk beside mine, wouldn't look up from it, pretending she found the desktop too endlessly fascinating to tear her eyes away from it.

Chapter Fifteen: The Sign on The Phone Pole

On an early April Saturday Mrs. Fujiwara made an exception to her no-more-movies rule for Emi. She said yes to Emi accompanying me to see Carole Lombard's last film, *To Be or Not To Be*. Emi was still wearing sunglasses whenever she went outside, concealing her eyes, and we had to take streetcars to get there rather than walk, but at least we were together at a movie again.

I almost liked President Roosevelt again when he said that Carole Lombard was "the first casualty of World War II," since she had died coming home from selling war bonds. I had to wonder how many more people wouldn't be coming home due to the war. If Emi hadn't been my best friend, I might have really hated the Japanese for starting it. But no, I could not hate them all. Maybe just the Emperor. He was the one in charge, so he had to be the one who agreed to let them attack us in the first place and started all this trouble.

Emi's mother approached mine the next day with an idea. Would it be possible for Emi to stay with Mom and me? Noriko had to be evacuated and couldn't possibly leave baby Hanae, who was only seven months old, but surely, she suggested, the authorities might be willing to let Emi stay with us. We were Americans, after all. So was Emi. That way Emi wouldn't have to leave our school.

I loved the idea, but secretly I had a feeling it would never work. Still, I said to Emi with a burst of enthusiasm, "That would be terrific!"

The idea perked Emi up considerably.

Mom naturally said of course it would be okay with her for Emi to stay with us. "But would it be allowable? That's the question. They want to remove *all* persons of Japanese ancestry, so let's not get our hopes up. Meanwhile, I'll call Colonel Barclay and ask him about this. I think if anyone would know if it's possible, he would."

I groaned. We had been blessed without the presence of Colonel Barclay for quite some time. He was back on active duty with the Army and I didn't miss having him around one bit, even if he had given me five whole dollars at Christmas.

I was relieved when Mom reached him by phone but didn't invite him and Madge to come over. "He said," she told me after hanging up, "it's absolutely *not possible* for us to consider keeping Emi. She's got to go away with the rest of them, no matter where they were born, here or there, or how old they are. It's outrageous, but there's not a thing we can do to change it."

I was getting tired of hearing so many adults saying that. True, there was nothing they could do, but shouldn't they try to *find* something?

"Is he the only authority in town, though, Mom? Can't you ask more people than just him? How about the mayor? Or the police chief? *Somebody* should be able to give us permission to keep her."

"I'll try, Ruby. But there are no guarantees. She's probably going to be evacuated no matter what we do." Mom sighed. "They all are."

* * * * *

Mom turned out to be right.

On March 23, 1942, General DeWitt issued Civilian Exclusion Order No. 1. It removed the Japanese families who lived on Bainbridge Island, Washington, a quiet community across Puget Sound, right near Seattle, to what was being called Puyallup Army Temporary Detention Center.

Detention Center? That sounded like a jail!

"It can't be that bad there," Mrs. Rivington tried to reassure us at school. "Before it was a detention center it was the Washington State Fairgrounds."

I'd been to the fair. It was always held on the same large stretch of land. Not much was there except for some permanent rides, including a roller coaster, and booths. Where were they going to put all of the Bainbridge Island Japanese people?

Mom actually saw quite a few of those very people being moved from the Bainbridge Island ferry to the train station on the day of their evacuation. She had been downtown shopping and had walked in the area of the station for no special reason. She stayed, with a whole crowd of onlookers, and couldn't help watching when the Japanese people came through. "They were quiet, but looked scared," she told me. "The Army was moving them along to their train and some had their guns out, pointed at them."

We looked at each other. Neither one of us said it but we both felt the Seattle Japanese would be told to move out next.

Dad faithfully wrote a letter to Mom and another to me, every single week. One day we got a rare letter addressed to us both together.

March 26, 1942

Fort Lewis

Dear Mary and Ruby,

Sorry to have to write you both in one letter but I have some good news and wanted to share it immediately. I'm going to Carlisle Barracks, Pennsylvania for additional training! I got selected for the division I most wanted to join and will leave Fort Lewis soon, but am not sure of the exact date yet. The minute I'm there you'll hear from me.

Onward and upward to victory!

Love,

Frank/Dad

"Pennsylvania? What kind of training can he be going there for?" I asked Mom. "And why doesn't he say?"

"Who knows?" Mom shrugged. "Perhaps they told him not to speak of it yet. 'Loose lips sink ships' and all that." That was a popular war slogan we were seeing these days on lots of posters and ads. It reminded us not to reveal anything about whatever the heck we knew concerning the war effort, not even to one another, since who knew if some innocent-looking person was really an honest-to-goodness spy and might overhear it? America had become a nation constantly afraid that spies could pop up everywhere. On the other hand, we probably had to be, since there was a war on. It was all so confusing. Whatever Dad's new division was, it might be disastrous for our servicemen if any of the Three Stooges of the Axis, Hitler, Mussolini and Hirohito, found out about it. Maybe Dad was even doing something top secret. I liked that idea! It appealed to me a lot.

"What a shame on the timing, though," said Mom. "I was hoping they'd let him come home for Easter, on leave."

"So was I."

Later, lying in bed that night, I thought of Dad's closing line again. *Onward and upward to victory.* Dad never signed a letter like that before. He always signed "with love." Was it just a fluke, or a clue? *Upward.* Maybe the new division had something to do with planes, or perhaps even zeppelins. Those looked like big fat giant-sized balloons and people could ride in them.

214

Two weeks later, right before Easter, Uncle Leo Manteffel took Mom to get her driver's license. She passed the test with flying colors.

Emi's mother wanted to get hers someday, too, but had decided to hold off. The way so many people thought the Japanese were spies and saboteurs, she didn't think the time was right for her to register as someone who wanted to drive. The atmosphere was just nuts.

Mrs. Rivington got a big surprise right before Easter and it wasn't a chocolate bunny or even a colorful egg. It was her son, Billy Rivington! He had been sent home from the hospital where he'd been recovering in Hawaii. He walked with crutches, but he could walk, and his doctors were hopeful that someday he'd get to throw the crutches away. He came to school to thank us in person for the cards we'd made him and brought the whole class cupcakes. That was a fun, almost-normal day.

Then finally, it happened a day later. The same terrible order they'd received on Bainbridge Island was proclaimed in Seattle. It appeared on notices stuck to telephone poles and bulletin boards all over town on a gray-sky Tuesday, April 21st. The bad news came from the Western Defense Command and Fourth Army Civil Control Administration. What a mouthful! The heading screamed in bold black letters:

INSTRUCTIONS TO ALL PERSONS OF JAPANESE ANCESTRY

Daisy, Vera, Emi and I had been trying to imitate the creepy voice of our favorite crime-fighting radio character, *The Shadow,* when we spotted one of the notices on a phone pole. The sky was darkening. We'd been walking at a fast pace, trying to hurry home from school to beat the rain that was surely on the way, from the looks of it.

We stopped at the phone pole to read one of them. It made me furious, balling my hands into fists, and poor Emi turned paler than I'd ever seen her as we absorbed the awful words.

It was even worse than we thought.

The notice said the head of every Japanese household and single Japanese adults had to report to an office over that very weekend to register and get "additional information." The Japanese would to be processed for evacuation, beginning in a few more days.

A list of things they needed to bring with them fell at the bottom of the notice. They could only take what they could carry, but were required to bring extra clothing, toilet articles, medicine, knives, forks, spoons, plates, bowls, cups, and "bedding and linens (no mattress)" – for *each* member of the family.

'How much room," I said, "can they have left in their suitcases for their clothes, or anything else, if they have to bring all that other stuff?"

"Oh, this is bad," Daisy breathed.

Then, worst of all, at the end of the notice came the words, "No pets will be allowed."

At that, Emi pointed to the words and let out a high-pitched cry that sounded more like a scream. "'No pets allowed?' What do they mean, they're not allowed? What's going to happen to my dog, my little Scottie, Buddy? My *Buddy!*"

The dog! Whoever would have thought they – I mean, we, the Americans, that is, - would really ban the Japanese people from the West Coast in the first place, let alone not even allow them to bring their own pets to join them? Everything was becoming crazier by the minute.

"I love Buddy. I could watch over him for you," I offered.

Emi, who had taken one blow after another rather quietly ever since Pear Harbor happened, suddenly became completely hysterical, sobbing loudly as we trudged along the street. Daisy and I walked on either side of her, each putting an arm around her.

Vera said, "In Berlin, Nazis - signs put up - too. Rules against Jews. This reminds me – of that. Against Jews there, Japanese here."

I shook my head. "I hate World War Two," I said emphatically.

"*You* hate it?" Emi pulled away from Daisy and me and whirled to face me as if I had just said something horrible. I'd never seen her look so mad. She pulled off her sunglasses and flung them into the gutter, where they shattered. Her dark eyes were blazing as she faced me. "How do you think *I* feel? I'm considered a Jap, a Slant-Eyes, a Yellow Belly, a Tojo, a Traitor – and worse! You, at least, don't have to go away like you're the enemy and get treated every day like you're a spy out to blow up America! I do. And it's not true! I have to leave just because that's what everyone else stupidly thinks of me, and everyone *is wrong!*"

"Everyone does not think that about you," I answered hotly. "I've never thought that of you in my life!"

"I haven't either," said Daisy. "Don't flip your lid at Ruby, Emi. It's not her fault this is happening."

"You look as Oriental as I do," Emi, who was crying some more, snapped at Daisy now, "but *you* won't have to go away!" I'd never seen my best friend get as upset as this.

"I left Berlin. Nazis there not like Jews," said Vera to her gently, trying to calm her. "Much better, get away from place they hate you."

"Your family *chose* to leave, though," Emi whirled on her furiously, now directing her anger at Vera. "We're not choosing it! We're being sent away like we're garbage that they can't wait to throw out."

"You're not garbage," I said firmly. "You're our friend Emi."

"No," my best friend replied, furiously wiping away her tears, "I'm Emiko, not 'Emi.' I've been thinking lately, how silly I've always been, calling myself 'Emi.' I thought it sounded more American, like 'Emily' or 'Emma,' and would help me fit in, since, let's face it, even before the war started I looked different from most people, so I stood out."

"I know exactly what you mean," agreed Daisy, nodding. "They don't, but I do."

"I know too," said Vera. "In Berlin, they hate me. Called me *'dreck.'* Means 'dirt.' For being Jewish."

I wondered if I should apologize for being the only one of us who didn't stand out because of my heritage. I was Irish-American, with a little bit of French ancestry thrown in from one great-grandfather. Lots of times I'd been called a 'loudmouth,' but nobody had ever called me names based on my complexion or said I was "dirt." If I had been growing up in another country where the majority of the people weren't white or Christian, or where folks who looked like me had launched an attack, wouldn't it have been me who was everyone's favorite target? It could happen to anybody.

Meanwhile, my friends still looked miserable, so I said in protest, "If you ask me, anyone who says such horrible things to any one of you is a complete idiot. It's all a bunch of malarkey! They're giving you bum raps and probably say that stuff without even knowing you. All three of you aren't dirt or bad or enemies or spies. That's insane, and whoever says such things can only be absolutely nuts!"

"Thanks, but..." Emi shook her head sadly. "In the long run what difference does it make? People still say it, and I'm being sent away anyway just because my parents were born in Japan and I look Japanese. This whole country is full of people who hate Japan."

Well, there was nothing I could say to that except for what I said, which was the lame, "It isn't fair."

"I'm sorry," Emi said softly, "for yelling at all of you. I'm just so mad about this."

I said, "We understand. Emiko."

At that point the dark sky started to empty little raindrops on our town, so we hurried home to our houses before the storm got any worse.

Chapter Sixteen: Keep Your Songs in Your Heart

Emiko's mother and baby sister were over at my house the next afternoon. Mom served Noriko tea to try and calm her down. My best friend's mom was hysterical. The baby was fussing, so I picked her up and rocked her, which only made her let out a long cry.

"Give her to me," Emi suggested, and I passed the baby along to her. She held her extra tight, singing to her softly, the song I'd heard her sing a long time ago at the Japanese school.

Mrs. Fujiwara had a tear-stained face and was more upset that day than I had ever seen her. "One week," she was wailing. "We have just one week to pack! We can only take what we can carry. They want us to sell what we cannot take, like the car and house. A man came by today. He said he would give me five hundred dollars for my house. It is worth ten thousand!"

"That's not a man," said Mom with feeling, "it's a crook!"

"You didn't take the money, did you?" I asked. I wasn't sure what was worse, Mrs. Fujiwara getting gypped out of the price of her beautiful home or the idea of a thief moving in next door. It was all far too horrible to think about, either way, and it gave me a case of the heebie-jeebies.

"No," Mrs. Fujiwara said, "but I took his card. How can I sell the house in only one week? What if nobody else buys? I would have to call that man, and take the money, even though it is too low. What would my husband say if I say yes to that price?"

"He'd say you were doing the best you could possibly do under extraordinarily bad circumstances," Mom said practically.

I looked at her. An idea had just formed in my head that was so good I blurted it right out. "Why sell it at all? Mom, wouldn't it be better if we looked after it for them?"

"What? Oh, Ruby, don't be silly," Mom waved my comment away. Yet a moment later she said, "Hmmm," like maybe she was considering it.

"Why not? We could take care of it until they're back."

Emiko's mother smiled, just a tiny bit. "If any person should have my house, it is you, Mary. You, I trust. Rent it to people while we are away."

"No," my mother said firmly, "I couldn't possibly take your home out from under you. That's out of the question."

"Someone else will anyway," said Emiko, shrugging. "In a week!"

"What happens to house if we walk away without finding a buyer?" her mother asked mine. "Why not sign it over to you, instead of selling it to the crooked man?"

They went back and forth discussing it, which took some time. In the end Mom decided t would be a great idea to take over the running of the Fujiwara house. There was a housing shortage in Seattle. We could fill the place up with workers from the Boeing plant. They kept pouring into town to take jobs and needed a place to stay. The house would get put in Mom's name for the duration of the war. Mom could run the house. I could help her. She and Noriko could split the rent money, they decided, but when the Fujiwaras came home, Mom would sign the house right back to them.

They decided they had a deal.

That's how Mom and I found ourselves in the boarding house business.

* * * * *

Most of the Japanese children stopped coming to school for the rest of that week, except for Paul and Sachiko who didn't miss a day. Emi stayed home to watch the baby and help her mother sort out what to take and what to put in storage. A lot of their better items like the good china, a piece of sculpture, their radio console and artwork found a new home in our small attic. They were relieved to know most of their furniture could be left in the house so the tenants could use it. As for the ice cream parlor, I asked Mr. Winbury for help. He promised to keep an eye on the place until the Fujiwaras came home.

Emi kept coming over to see me after school, sadly giving me her best games, beloved toys, books and even art supplies. There was no way she could take them all with her. She trusted me to look after her Japanese porcelain dolls, still stored in my room since the day the FBI came to her house, until after the war. "I'm taking my notebook with my list of *Hit Parade* songs in it, though," she said. "No matter what, that's coming with me, even if I have to stuff it down my shirt."

I tried to laugh. "Let's hope it won't come to that."

Emi shrugged. "It would give me more of a figure than I've got already. Mama suggested I wear more than one blouse on the day we leave. Nuts, right? But it would free up extra space in my suitcase if I do."

That Saturday we walked Emi's blue Schwinn bicycle over to Vera Manteffel's house. Emi had wanted to give it to me, since it was only a year old, but I already had a bike and we knew Vera didn't. "She'll probably be your new best friend now," Emi said miserably. "She's nice and sure can sing. You two could be the new Gemstone Girls all by yourselves."

"If we are, it will only be until you're back and then we *three* will be the Gemstone Girls."

Emi managed to smile at that.

Later we went over to Daisy's house with several almost-new pretty dresses that Emi had nearly outgrown. Daisy, whose arm was now out of the sling, was a size smaller than Emi. Some of Emi's ritziest dresses wound up in happy Daisy's closet.

Buddy, the dog, accompanied us on both of the deliveries, then over to my house. I wasn't sure what was going to happen on Tuesday morning when poor Emi had to leave him behind. "You'll take good care of Buddy, won't you?" she asked me, as our favorite radio show was about to start on Saturday night.

"Of course. Count on it."

"We'll give him lots of love, but we're just minding him for you until you can come back home," Mom, who had come into the room, assured Emi. But the dog was already about eight years old, almost a geezer in dog years. Who knew when the Fujiwaras would be back, and how old he might be by then?

We settled back on the armchairs in my living room to listen, together one final time, to *Your Hit Parade*, Emi with her marble notebook out, her dark red fountain pen ready to record the hits. It seemed like such a normal Saturday night, but it wasn't. To make matters worse, the number one song in the country that week was "Somebody Else is Taking My Place." It made Emi burst out crying.

"Oh, Emi," I said, trying to reach over to give her a pat on the back, but I didn't get the chance. She picked up Buddy and the notebook and rushed home, sobbing her heart out, so upset she forgot her best pen.

"Let her go," Mom advised. "That sweet little girl probably needs to cry a whole ocean of sadness out of her system tonight."

"Oceans," I said, "are the whole problem, aren't they? If her parents hadn't crossed one to come here…maybe I never would have known her, but she wouldn't be caught in a trap like this, either. Not if she was growing up in Tokyo or Kyoto, or some city in Japan."

"And to think," said Mom, "her parents came here to make a better life."

"Now he's in jail and they're getting sent away. Coming here made everything worse."

On Monday all of the nine Japanese students from my class who were about to be removed from Seattle came back to school at our kind-hearted teacher's request. Mrs. Rivington had decreed we would give them a royal send-off and as always she proved true to her word. She brought a strawberry shortcake from the bakery and green glass bottles of Coca-Cola for everybody. She also told us to feel free to bring our autograph books to school, something that we normally only did at the end of the year, so we could write goodbye messages to one another in them.

After distributing the cake slices she said, "There's really no way to make this unhappy day any easier, children. Everyone here's either sad to be going away or sad to see you leave."

Except Barbara, who couldn't wait.

Mrs. Rivington went on, "I personally can't bear it that my Japanese students will be going away today. But I do know one thing, and it's that nothing lasts forever," she assured us. "What's inside-out today can be right-side-up again tomorrow. It's getting through it until then that's going to be your challenge, but you can meet it."

She passed around sheets paper with the name on top of every child who was leaving. They were passed from desk to desk and we wrote our addresses on them so our soon-to-be-former classmates could write to us and keep in touch. Mrs. Rivington wrote her address on each of sheet, too.

I brought the camera with me that last day and took plenty of pictures. Mrs. Rivington with Emi. Sachiko, Mariko, Emi and Violet. Annie Sanderson with her best friend, Momoko. The "Three Musketeers," Paul Yamaguchi and his best buddies since second grade, Christopher Callavari and Tatsuo Gima. The Hasegawa twins, Marcie and Mark, with Sylvia Lindstrom.

Mrs. Rivington had made awards certificates for each of the nine. Paul got "Class Clown." Emi was "Class Light Beam." Sachiko, who was a straight-A student, got "#1 Genius." She saved Tatsuo, the boy who had told people he was Chinese so that he wouldn't have to take any flak for being Japanese, for last. He got "Best Actor." Finally we had a reason to laugh.

"I was afraid you'd give me Class Liar," he said. "At least I won't have to pretend to be what I'm not where we're going."

When Miss Bryce, our teacher from the fifth grade who had been such a toughie, came into the room to say goodbye to the kids who were leaving, she shocked us by starting to cry. "What they're doing to you is downright unconstitutional," she told them, sounding out of control. "You mark my words! There will be a day of reckoning for America about what they're doing to you children! You Seattle kids are *our* children. They have no right sending any single one of you away without a trial!"

The whole class was stunned. It had always been obvious that Mrs. Rivington loved us, but it was absolutely astonishing to see Miss Bryce, of all people, in tears over the evacuation. She was always such a grouch. We never even realized she *liked* any of us before this moment, but, clearly, she didn't just like us. She *loved* us, and enough to be more obviously upset than any of the rest of the faculty. "They should let you stay," she cried on, miserably. It caused Emi, along with Marcie Hasegawa, to break down and start to cry. Emi's tears were silent ones. Marcie sobbed out loud.

Mr. Winbury came into our classroom just then to find out what was causing Miss Bryce to flip her wig so loudly. She carried on even further, saying something about how the removal of the Japanese was ripping our whole community apart. I was about to agree when I heard the principal say urgently to her in a low voice, "I know this is awful, it's tearing me in pieces too, but for the children's sake will you *please* calm down? Try to be positive for them. They're upset enough."

Mrs. Rivington, fingering her pearl necklace and with tears in her own eyes that she blinked away, had to usher Miss Bryce out before she got into even more of an uproar. I think it was in desperation that she spotted Vera and said to her, "You've been through this twice already, darling. You left homes in Berlin and Paris. Do you have any advice you can give to your classmates before they go?"

Vera thought for a few moments. "Yes, but - can someone get Max? I am - not sure - how to say it."

"I'll go," I volunteered. I was happy to leave my classroom for the few seconds it took to get Max from his, two doors down the hall. It was easier to breathe once I got out of that room.

Max came back and spoke to Vera in German and English for about a minute. Then she said to the class, "Okay, here is what I want say. I had big house in Germany. Nice room. Music boxes. Piano, record player, records. When they say we move, I can't get all in suitcase."

Several of the Japanese children smiled at that and nodded. They'd spent the past week trying to stuff things they loved in their suitcases. Only one suitcase apiece.

"My father say, can't bring music boxes. Can't bring piano. Can't bring what not fit in suitcase. But he say, 'You can keep your songs in your, ah, *herz*.'"

"Heart, Vera," said Max. "'*Herz*' is heart."

"Heart," smiled Vera. "Keep your songs in your heart. Don't forget your songs. Even if you go where they sing *anders*."

"*Anders* means 'different ones,'" said Max. "Others."

"Different ones," repeated Vera. "You bring your own songs with you."

"That's beautiful, Vera!" Mrs. Rivington told her. "You mean your memories, too, am I right? You take your memories, your songs, your heritage and your culture, your likes and favorites and all the good things that you are, right along with you wherever you go."

"Yes! *Genau!*"

"That means 'exactly,'" translated Max.

"Take the poems, prayers and the quotes you love along too," Mrs. Rivington added, since she loved all three. I think quotes were her favorite things, the way songs were mine and Emi's and Vera's. "Keep them in your hearts and they'll never leave you, or let you down, either. We cannot control everything that happens to us, but -"

Tatsuo interrupted her with, "You can say that again!" A few students laughed.

"We can't control it all, but we can do our best to take charge of our own hearts, minds and attitudes," our teacher ruffled his hair and went on. "Prayers, songs and quotes have the power to lift your spirits, and those of the people you love, too, if only you give them the chance."

"Good advice," said Paul Yamaguchi. "But I'm taking my saxophone for real, not just in my heart, and in a music case."

"That's good, too," said Max. He shook hands with some of the boys before he returned to his classroom.

"Brava, Vera!" Mr. Winbury smiled. "You may be a child who's still learning our language, but that was one beautiful sentiment to impart." She didn't fully understand what he meant but smiled uncertainly.

Before the final bell rang, Mrs. Rivington said, "I know those of you who leave this week will be fine wherever you land, but I'm hoping you can come home soon!" This time the tears she'd been fighting back all afternoon began to fall. "And, and," her voice faltered as she wiped the tears away, "hitch your wagons to a star, and keep your songs in your hearts."

It took a long time for us to leave the building that day. Nobody left immediately except Barbara, which was a first, since my classmates and I always burst out the door whenever the bell rang, but this time we knew we were about to be split apart. What, I wondered, looking around the room, would it be like to come back to school and no longer have so many of these friends since kindergarten here? *Why* did this have to happen? The children who were being sent away wanted a few more minutes with their friends who were staying, and also with Mrs. Rivington. Those of us not being evacuated couldn't bear to leave either.

"Remember when you used to say that Ruby and I might one day have an act?" Emi, in a tiny voice, asked our teacher, when it was her turn to talk to her.

"Of course, Emi!" Mrs. Rivington put her hands on Emi's shoulders.

"Do you, do you still believe it?" Emi asked, starting to weep.

"I not only still believe it," our teacher assured her, "I plan on being there for your opening night! Good things will still happen to my sparkling little Emerald. Amazing things. You're an effervescent girl, Emi. I trust when you get where you're going you'll do what you can to brighten things up for everybody around you, just like you've been doing here all year." Our teacher hugged her tight. "But you can't imagine just how much I wish this wasn't happening, and you could stay right here, where you belong. I'll miss you so."

"Emiko, I'll stop by to speak with your mother tonight," Mr. Winbury said as we were going out the main door of the school together for the last time. That was about the Fujiwara's ice cream parlor. "I found someone who can look after your father's shop for you."

Emi came over to my house before it was time for me to leave for school on Tuesday morning, the day of their departure. She carried Buddy in her arms, holding the dog as gently as she usually did her little sister.

"I know you'll be great with him," she said, her voice no more than a flat whisper because she was trying not to cry. "He knows you, so he won't be afraid to stay here." She handed her pet to me. I could tell her heart was breaking to let him go.

Mom came outside, trying not to cry, and gently took the dog from my arms. She quickly brought him inside, not wanting to prolong the sad moment for Emi's sake.

"We'll watch over him until you come back," I promised.

"We don't know if we'll ever come back, actually," Emi said miserably.

"Of course you'll be back. We're taking care of the house for you too. Nothing lasts forever, Mrs. Rivington said yesterday. Remember? Not even wars."

"With my luck, who knows? This just one might. You'd better write to me." Emi tried to perk up a bit and almost managed a smile.

So did I, but there were tears in my eyes. "You better believe it, my Emerald Gemstone Sister, I sure will." I handed her the pen she'd left in my house Saturday night. "You need this back."

Mom came outside and told me I didn't have to go right to school that morning. "You can go in late today. I think it would be nice if you came too when I drive the Fujiwaras over to Belltown." That was a Seattle neighborhood. It was where buses had been arranged to transport evacuees to Puyallup Detention Center.

Emi really was wearing two skirts, *three* blouses, a sweater and a coat so that she could take more of her nicest clothes with her. "Do you really have the *Hit Parade* notebook with you under your collection of blouses?" I pulled her aside and asked, out of our mother's earshot.

"No, I didn't have to. I laid it flat in my suitcase after I took out these," gesturing to the extra clothes she had on, "and it fit. I got my autograph book and the address list for of our classmates in there, too."

I noticed there was a tag tied through a buttonhole on Emi's coat. It had her name on it, her destination – Puyallup - and also her "Family Number."

"Did you ever see the glamorous Marlene Dietrich wearing anything as bad as *this* in a movie?" She twirled it around her finger and tried to laugh it off, but the smile didn't wipe out the sad expression that stayed in her yes. "They're forcing us evacuees to wear tags until we get there, on top of everything else. The baby's got one pinned onto her little outfit, too."

Children were wearing tags on their way to a detention center? This country, I thought, has gone completely nuts.

That's when Vera arrived to say goodbye to the Fujiwaras. "Oh, glad you're here – I have something for you," Emi said, running back into the house for a minute.

Noriko came out of the house carrying the baby, gave her to Mom, and went back in to get two suitcases. She gave my mother the keys to her house.

Emi came out carrying the music box shaped like a gramophone that had been in her living room for as long as I knew her, the one that played "The Blue Danube Waltz." "Thought you might like to have this," she said to Vera. "There's no room for it in my suitcase, and you had to leave all your old music boxes behind. I think you should have this as the start of a new collection."

"Thank you," Vera smiled, but there were tears in her yeas. "You are so nice. I will miss you, Emi." They hugged. I wished Vera could come to the assembly point with us but she had to go off to school.

Mom ushered the rest of us into the car, Dad's good old DeSoto.

We were all pretty silent during the short drive, except for the baby, who cried a lot up front with Mom and Noriko. Sitting next to Emi behind them, I thought of the first day we'd gone together to Kindergarten. She had been more frightened that day than I had, but we were fine because we'd gone into school for the first time together. I though she must have been terribly scared today, too, a whole lot more than she would ever admit, not knowing for certain what was coming next. But I couldn't go with her this time.

Wherever they send her, I silently prayed to God, *please let her be all right. Let all our friends stay safe.*

I thought of what Dad had said to me the night before he left for basic training. "Wherever you go, we'll see the same sun rising in the morning and the same moon every night, there as here. That'll connect us. Seattle and all your friends in it will still be here when you get back," I told her.

Emi nodded.

Outside, it rained on and off. There was some morning rush hour traffic, but I still felt we arrived at the assembly point too soon.

Once there, in the middle of the crowd of Japanese people and umbrellas, I spotted the last person I ever wanted to see: Colonel Barclay. He seemed to be one of the officers assisting with the evacuation. Wouldn't you know it?

"Mary, Ruby!" He exclaimed, "What a surprise to see you here." I was afraid he'd make a snide remark, but for once, he didn't. He looked over at Noriko, struggling to cart a suitcase, a cloth bag of additional possessions, and Hanae, too. "And these are your friends," he said, with more kindness in his voice than I ever would have imagined he had in him, especially for Japanese people. "Come, let me help you," he said to Nori, and checked their names against a list. Then he brought her suitcase, and Emi's, too, over to a waiting bus.

Get right on," he told them, "you don't want to be out in this rain with a baby."

Noriko, crying miserably, hugged my mother quickly. I hugged Emi and kissed baby Hanae's sweet little face. I could hear my mother telling Emi to make sure she kept on singing. Then, too fast, they boarded their bus, disappearing inside. One second they were here, the next, gone from view.

"Thanks for being so nice to them. Will you be going to Puyallup, too?" I asked Colonel Barclay.

"Yes," he said, "though not today. After the evacuation is complete, later this week, I'll be stationed there."

"Will you please keep an eye on them for me, Colonel?" I asked, with tears running down my face.

"Of course, Ruby. Oh, my good girl, don't cry. Please don't cry. I know you think this is horrible, what the Army has been asked to do here today, but it's necessary. It's a casualty of the war." Then he surprised me by letting out a sigh. "But it's a crying shame, too! There's so many Japanese *children* here. I never realized how many there would be." He looked rather shocked about it.

"Yes, and they're all considered possible spies, too, right?" I couldn't help but add hotly as I wiped my face with a handkerchief Mom had handed me. "That baby, Hanae, is seven months old. Do they really think she's *spy material?*"

237

The colonel stuttered and sputtered but couldn't answer that. Well maybe I'd given him something to think about.

"Oh, look! Their cousins are over there. The Kimuras." I smiled and waved at Molly, Nicky and their mother. They didn't return the smile but waved back. "Would you watch out for them, too?"

"You! You'll ask me to look out for every Japanese from Seattle, next," Colonel Barclay grumped, which made him sound more like his usual self. "But okay, let me get those Kimuras of yours loaded onto the bus." True to his word, he went over and helped them, carrying two of their bags.

Mr. Winbury came by to talk to former students and parents. He took Paul Yamaguchi's suitcase for him. Paul had been struggling with his suitcase in one hand and his saxophone case in the other. Our Father Murphy, who only had a few Japanese parishioners, nevertheless was there, too, offering words of encouragement and giving people blessings.

Mom and I stayed at the edge of the crowd for the next few hours, in the rain, shivering under an umbrella. Sachiko and Violet, from my class, were there, waiting for instructions to board their bus. They waved to me, but then were lost in the crowd. Finally the engine of the bus that the Fujiwaras and Kimuras were riding on pulled away from the curb. They weren't able to see we were still outside. Someone on the bus had pulled every shade down, covering the windows so they couldn't see where they were eaded, which was as crazy as anything else that had gone on lately, considering we

lready knew they were going to Puyallup. Mom and I waved anyway, hoping Emi or

ne of the others lifted the shade, until the bus with our friends was gone. I didn't cry

until it was out of sight. Then it was hard to stop.

Chapter Seventeen: Nine Empty Desks

I didn't go to school that day after all. Mom changed her mind about sending me in.

"Don't cry so, Ruby. I think they'll be okay, wherever they're taken. What a thing to have happen!"

"Something major is wrong in the world," I sniffled, "for this to be taking place at all."

"That's the truth! I so wish somebody could have stopped this from happening. Meanwhile, believe it or not, life will go on, my sweet girl," said Mom kindly, "and I think we've seen enough misery for one day."

"You sure have," agreed Mr. Winbury, coming over to join us. "And your mother is absolutely right. Life will go on, and one day our Japanese friends will be home. So will our soldiers. In the meantime, you heard what Vera Manteffel said yesterday, didn't you, about keeping your songs in your heart?"

I nodded, wiping away the latest tear.

"You have to do that, too, Ruby."

"Why? It's not like I'm packing up to go away. Mom and I are staying right here."

"Yes, you are, and thank goodness for that, since so many folks I know are either joining the service like your father or being sent away like Emi. I'm beginning to think one day I'll wake up in Seattle and not know anyone who's left. But the rest of us have got to stand firm and hold on to everything we know is right and good, now more than ever. All the people we love who have gone away are going to be counting on us to stay right on the beam until they get back home." He nodded to my mother and turned back to me. "See you in school tomorrow, Ruby, and remember what I said."

A soft breeze came out of nowhere, messing up my bangs. "Yes, Mr. Winbury, I will."

After the principal walked away, Mom said, "You must be hungry. Let's go out for hamburgers," she suggested, "and then would you maybe, by any chance, like to go to the movies?"

I brushed another tear away. "Well, I'd never say no to that." I didn't add that it hardly felt fair for us to be having a nice day out while our friends were riding on a bus to get locked away simply for coming from the same background as Hirohito. Mom was determined to cheer us both up, which was a really nice thing for her to do. She drove the car to the Igloo Drive-In Restaurant, which looked like something out of a book about Eskimos, and ordered sodas and "Igloo Burgers." Later we saw *The Courtship of Andy Hardy* starring Mickey Rooney.

Emi's little dog Buddy was happy to see us when we got home. He even greeted us with his tail wagging. "You're the silver lining in the cloud of this whole evacuation, Buddy," I told him. "It's really going to be nice to have you stay with us."

That night I found the strip of two photos of Emi and me that we'd taken months ago in the brand new booth at Mr. Fujiwara's ice cream parlor right before the attack. I propped it against a framed photo of Dad in his uniform that I kept on my dresser. Every day I could see the photos. Strange. One day they'd both been here. Now they were gone away, and it almost seemed like Daddy and Emi the people had been changed into Daddy and Emi the memories.

The next day, entering my classroom, I was shocked to see so many empty desks where the Japanese students used to sit. Nine sad-looking desks without their students had been moved to one side of the room.

Mrs. Rivington came in and wasn't happy with the sight either. "What are *those* still doing there? I told the janitor to remove them yesterday." She seemed angry at first, then ready to cry, and finally rushed out of the room for a few moments. I had the feeling she didn't want us to see her upset again like on the Japanese kids' last day. When she came back, sure enough, her face was tear-stained. She said to us briskly, "Come on, children, I've cleared it with the principal, and you're going to visit the school library for awhile." It wasn't our day or time to go, but off we went down the hall to visit the small room full of books that served as a library.

Once back in the classroom, we found the janitor had removed the nine desks. It was amazing to see how much extra space we had, now that there were only sixteen students in our room instead of twenty-five. Without being told to do so, we moved our remaining desks around to try to fill up the room.

Mrs. Rivington said, "Children, I have to say, the circumstances we find ourselves in at the moment are as strange as they come. I didn't want to mention this when the Japanese children were still here, but I never thought America would *ever* round up any group of children as virtual prisoners of war, and for no reason. Especially children who were born here! I want to urge all of you to keep in touch with our missing friends. Let them know we still care, no matter what those in the government and the public happen to be saying about them. We know them, so we know those 'spy' accusations are untrue."

The corners of my mouth turned upward, almost into a smile, when the teacher said that. I was more tired than I could ever explain from hearing that so many wonderful people I knew were "potential spies" just because their families came from Japan.

"Meanwhile," Mrs. Rivington continued, "the rest of us may be a much smaller class, but we're still *a class*. I think we need to start the day off with a fun activity this morning." Then she decided we should have a Geography Bee instead of a geography lesson, the girls against the boys, so our first day without our Japanese classmates began with a friendly competition. Mrs. Rivington named the country. We had to guess the continent. The girls won. Later that afternoon she divided us in teams of four to make victory banners for the school hallways, putting me together with Vera, Sylvia and Annie Sanderson. I think our teacher was trying her best to help us make stronger connections with the kids who were still there. I hardly knew Annie, who had been as close with her friend Momoko as I'd been with Emi, but I liked her. She seemed terribly sad that day to be there without her best pal. I certainly knew the feeling and made a point of telling her I was glad to have her on my team. Annie smiled like I'd just handed her a present.

It seemed to take forever before I heard from Emi. I wrote her twice before I heard anything back, two long weeks later.

10 May 1942

Puyallup

Dear Ruby,

So sorry it's taken me so long to write you! I already got the two letters you sent.

You should see this place! Camp Puyallup is part big adventure and part squirrel cage. "Very primitive," the adults call it. Means it's tougher than the campgrounds in Yosemite were, even though there, we were in a tent with sleeping bags, and believe it or not that was more comfortable than this.

We got off the buses here after about an hour on the first day and lined up to get medical exams and then be assigned to our "living quarters." We thought they would give us an apartment or a nice room. What dumbbells we were. Well, you aren't going to believe it, but do you know what Mama, my baby sister and I were given to live in? A HORSE STALL!

That's what they already had here, horse's stalls from when this was used as the fairgrounds, but which clod in the Army decided to have people live in them? They've also built lots of wooden barracks that actually don't look much better.

There were three empty bed frames waiting for us in the stall. Mama sent me to fill three burlap sacks we were given with straw to make a "mattress." Hanae's really too small for a whole bed so later I was sent outside again to find a wooden crate that we covered with some bath towels we'd brought with us to make her a cradle. Well, sort of. Some cradle! And now we're short on towels because there's only one left for all three of us.

Mama says we've got to try to make the best of things since we have no other choice, so I'm trying. It's not easy. She also said we need to show "the Americans" (as if I'm not one) what good and dignified people we are so that they'll start to believe it. To that I say, why don't they show us how great they are so that we can believe it? Mama doesn't know how to answer that.

We're glad about one thing. We have Aunt Hinako Kimura right here in the horse stall next door, with Nicky and Molly. Some families have their relatives clear on the other side of the camp. Nicky and Molly had me go out with them again to help with the bales of straw where we made their "mattresses." I couldn't help saying that between the stalls and the hay, we're being treated like horses here, so we might as well all neigh. That got us all laughing and making neighing noises, too, until some of the older Japanese adults said we should stop it and "take it in silence." I said if I have to take it, I'd rather make some noise.

We sneaked over to the area of the former fairgrounds where the roller coaster and the other rides are. They're not in operation, though I can't understand why not. The least they could do is give us kids free rides on the rides, but they don't. It was fun to go where we weren't supposed to until one of the guards found us and yelled like mad.

Oh, we don't have any kind of school set up here yet. I wish we did.

I want to go home!!!!!!!

I miss you.

Emi

P.S.: If one more adult here says, "Shikata ga nai," Japanese for "It cannot be helped," I'm going to scream. This could've been helped, but it's everybody's favorite camp saying. I could scream every time somebody says it. I mean it. You'll hear me. And you live over an hour away.

I was so relieved to hear from her. I'd been wondering if they arrived there in one piece. Barbara Andrews had been spreading rumors that the Japanese weren't really going to Puyallup at all, but would be shot dead on the way. I was happy to see she was wrong again. As soon as I got the note I wrote back to Emi.

Seattle

May 13, 1942

Dear Emi,

Are you kidding me? They have you living in a horse's stable? And there's adults running around saying "it can't be helped"? That's nuts! And not letting you kids ride the roller coaster is crazy, too. Those things are built to be ridden, not to just sit there.

I'd revolt if I were you. Right now, this minute!

Glad to hear you've been neighing about the stables and the straw in the beds. Keep it up! It should drive those in charge of the camp batty. The whole setup sounds crazy.

What do you mean, there's no school there?

Buddy is fine but I know he misses you. Whenever I put him on a leash and take him for a walk he tries to pull me in the direction of your house. For now it's sad to watch but I keep telling him one day you'll be home.

I miss you too,

Ruby

P.S.: Enclosed in this package are new pretty pink bath towels Mom and I got for you, your mother and Hanae – enjoy! Let us know what else we can send you.

There wasn't a response for about a month. Mrs. Rivington, who was also anxious to hear from her former pupils at Puyallup, told us that The Office of Censorship checked the mail first, in both directions, before sending it on to the recipients or back to us, so that no vital information about the war could be leaked - to enemies. For heaven's sake!

As my mother had promised, life went on, although during wartime it didn't ever feel entirely normal. I could never fully get used to the odd fact that so many people were suddenly missing from our lives, and not just gone but scattered in so many different directions. They should have all been home.

Mom and I rented Emi's house to fifteen young women who came to Seattle to help the war effort. They found jobs in the Boeing plant that made military aircraft. That was some plant! Eventually it was even camouflaged so that if the Japanese or the Nazis flew over Seattle in an air raid they wouldn't realize it was a plane factory. It was made to look like city streets! The girls were a lively bunch and unofficially adopted me as their little sister. They taught me more about clothing styles and makeup than I'd ever known before and there was always some intrigue going on with the girls' various romance problems.

That spring I especially loved a new movie, *Mrs. Miniver*. Greer Garson starred as a wife and mother in England who was going through all kinds of chaos due to this war. I elt very lucky to be living so far away from Europe after I saw it. The Nazi Luftwaffe – that was their air force – flew over England on a regular basis to drop bombs on factories, airfields, shipyards, and ordinary English people who were just trying to live their lives.

For a few weeks after Emi left, I didn't have the heart to listen to "Your Hit Parade" without her there beside me. It seemed so disloyal. Mom told me I was being silly and that avoiding my favorite program wasn't going to either reverse the President's proclamation about sending the Japanese away or get Emi released from Puyallup, but at first I just couldn't bear to listen to the show. Finally my mother invited Vera over one Saturday night, specifically to hear the program with me, and I gave in for Vera's sake. "Tangerine" made it to the number one song of the week. She sang along with the radio, I joined in, and some of the fun was back.

Meanwhile, the strangest school year I'd ever had finally ended. I left the sixth grade with good marks in every subject but math, as usual. I had loved truly being in Mrs. Rivington's class. She was my favorite teacher of them all, so on the last day I stayed behind when all the other kids flew out the door to begin their summer. I helped her put away the books, chalk, erasers and supplies. Together we took down all the cheery quote signs she had on the walls, to be kept until the next term started.

Miss Bryce popped into the room to say goodbye for the summer. "Have you heard from Emiko, Ruby?" She asked me, looking concerned.

"Yes, I got a letter from her."

"Is she doing okay?"

"Well, it sounds like she's all right, for the most part, but the conditions in Puyallup are horrible. They assigned Emi, her mother and the baby to living quarters in a horse's stable."

"They *what?*" Miss Bryce shrieked.

"It makes me ashamed of my country," Mrs. Rivington sighed, "when I hear of incidents like that. And this isn't the only one. Paul Yamaguchi's family's staying in a horse stall too."

Miss Bryce shook her head. "I heard people are calling those Puyallup fairgrounds 'Camp Harmony.' Harmony? What kind of *harmony* can there be when they're putting children in horse stalls? On top of the indignity of it, they could all end up with pneumonia!"

"You know Emi," I added. "It's horrible, yet it's all bringing out her fighting spirit."

"It shouldn't have to!" Miss Bryce grumbled. "I've said it before and I'm saying it again, Ruby, what's been done to our Japanese friends and neighbors is dead wrong. It's only a matter of time before the whole matter comes to a head. Meanwhile, I'm going to visit friends who have a house in Lake Tapps for a few weeks, deliberately, because it's right ear Puyallup. I want to visit the place and see if there's something I can do for the kids rom our school and their families."

That's a great idea!"

You know, I'd liberate them from that place myself if I could. As a matter of fact, nothing would give me greater pleasure than to ride into that Camp Harmony, behind the wheels of a tank, and set them all free." On that note, she turned on the heels of her ugly black shoes and all but marched out of the classroom.

"Our Miss Bryce on a tank. Now wouldn't *that* just be a vivid sight," Mrs. Rivington winked at me.

For the first time in weeks, I let out a great big belly laugh.

Chapter Eighteen – Home Front Days

Summer that year was a lot of fun because I went with the Manteffel family to their beach house and stayed for two whole months. It was relaxing to wake up every day with the sound of the ocean in my ears and to spend long mornings walking through the surf with Vera and Maximillian. Uncle Leo banned German in the house and asked me to converse in English with Max and Vera as much as possible. Mom said for once the fact that I loved to talk would be an asset. She stayed behind in Seattle, acting as a combination manager and den mother of the Boeing girls staying in the house next door, and visited the beach house every few weekends.

One night Vera woke up hysterical. I had my own tiny room, decorated with glass floats and curtains with anchor designs. Vera's room was down the hall, but she was so upset by her nightmare that everybody in the house was awakened by her cries. She'd had a bad dream about the days before the family left Berlin. In it, she told me the next day, she had been dragged down a boulevard by a bunch of kids, including some Hitler Youth boys, who were taking turns punching her. It had really happened. At the time, Vera had been ten years old, the bullies fourteen.

"As safe as my children are here," Rosi Manteffel said to me, "they're never going to fully feel like it, I'm afraid. Not after what happened there. Be proud your father joined up to fight the Nazis."

If he goes to Europe, that is," I said, since we still didn't know where my father was going to be stationed. He was still in training in Carlisle Barracks.

Wherever he gets sent, he joined to take a stand against their viciousness. That's fabulous."

By the time September rolled around Vera and I started the seventh grade tanned and refreshed from those days at the ocean. Our new teacher, Mrs. Throckmorton, was a funny Seattle transplant from Broken Arrow, Oklahoma who couldn't stop telling us stories about how much better The Sooner State was in comparison to Washington. It didn't sound that luxurious to me. The lady grew up bathing in a tin tub in the backyard because her folks didn't have plumbing in the house, and who could miss *that?*

I never heard so many stories about any place in my life as I did about Broken Arrow. I started to wish Mrs. Throckmorton would go back there just so I wouldn't have to hear anything more about that place every day. I missed being in Mrs. Rivington's class.

On another note, Jessup Marz was back at our elementary school for eighth grade because he'd been kicked out of the military academy his dad had enrolled him in the year before. *Nobody* ever gets kicked out of military school, but Jessup did. Chester Yang was overjoyed, but the rest of us groaned out loud on the first day back when we saw Jessup coming across the schoolyard. The rest of us joked about placing bets on how long it would take before those two got suspended again.

Camp Harmony/Puyallup of the Horse Stalls turned out to only a temporary measure. Emi, her mother and sister, and the rest of my former Japanese classmates were soon transferred away from there, but only to another camp, this one called Minidoka Relocation Center in Idaho, far away from the west coast, that September. They weren't allowed back home yet.

In one of her first letters from Minidoka Emi wrote that the new camp was "an improvement over the last one, though only by the tiniest little bit. We're lucky enough to be living with the Kimuras, not sharing our space with strangers, together in one room in a flimsy wood barracks building. But hey, at least it was built for people, not stallions and mares. There's other people here who were assigned to room with strangers they'd never met before in their lives."

There were three Fujiwaras and three Kimuras. There would have been four and four if the two fathers weren't still in jail. All quartered in one room! This was atrocious. I shook my head, unable to understand what the camp authorities thought they were doing.

Emi reported the room was heated by a "primitive kind of stove." Minidoka was far inland, steaming hot in the summer and freezing cold in winter. The camp was "so far removed from civilization that when you write me back, you should address the letter to me as 'Emiko Fujiwara, Minidoka Relocation Center, The Middle of Nowhere, Idaho.'"

Her letters made light of all kinds of camp matters yet still described unbearable conditions. It took a few months but schools finally opened at the camp – in November.

nstead of desks, the kids sat at wooden picnic tables created in the camp carpentry shop. "Too bad Jessup Marz isn't stuck out here too. Sometimes kids get splinters up heir rumps." A lot of the teachers hired to work there couldn't bear the conditions and eft immediately. Emi wrote, "They have the choice of leaving – we don't. Who can blame them?" The camp streets weren't paved but made of dirt, and could get terribly muddy after any rainstorm or, that winter, when the snow melted. "Some days I call the street where my barracks is located Quasi-Quicksand Boulevard." On the other hand, when they first arrived the place was sometimes plagued with dust storms, with dried dirt flying through the air on the wind and also managing to get through any and all crevices in the barracks buildings, landing on people as they slept. "Whoever thought flying dirt could be worse than a snowy blizzard? At least snow melts."

Just when I figured that camp wasn't too much better than living in the horse stall had been, Emi was quick to add to one of her first letters from there, in late November of 1942:

There are two things I can't help but like about being here, believe it or not. One is the mountain range we can see in the distance. They're snow-capped mountains, majestic and quite beautiful, like something out of a song. The other is the stars that shine above this place in the evenings, that look bigger and brighter and seem closer to earth than they ever did when we were home. It's even possible while walking along the dirt streets of the camp at night to feel you could reach up for one of those stars and grab it. And, like you said before we left, we've got the same over us during the day that also shines on Seattle, and we can see the same moon at night.

Ruby, some days I can hardly remember what living in Seattle was like. Can you believe it? Did I really once have a pretty blue and green bedroom in a house my family had all to ourselves? Really? All we have here are barracks, barracks and more barracks. And they're covered in black tarpaper, totally cheerless and ugly. What's wrong with the idea of using pink, blue and yellow paper instead?

Still, whenever I happen to be outside when night is falling and see the first star in the sky, I wish on it. You know what I wish for. I want to go home.

Oh well, I guess it could be worse. Those who keep saying "shikata ga nai"/"it cannot be helped" have got that right, even though I'm still sick of hearing it. It cannot be helped until we're let out of here.

It's almost Thanksgiving. Please give everyone my love.

Emi

That was Emi. She was living under miserable conditions yet she wanted me to give her regards to her old friends. Thanksgiving 1942 was so different from the one in 1941, not to mention that wonderful, unforgettable Sunday right after it, when we were told of the Hollywood plans and were thrilled at the whole idea. Hollywood…

By then Vera, who was a wonderful girl, had become my new best friend, but that didn't mean we forgot our old ones. Emi wrote to her, too. She was as mad and as shocked as I was by Emi's descriptions of life in Minidoka. So Vera and I decided it would be a ice idea to raise money for Christmas presents for every single one of our old classmates who had been sent there, and get some for their siblings, too. Annie, Sylvia, Daisy and Lynnie pitched in. We held three bake sales to get funds, one at school, one at Vera's synagogue, and one at my church. Mr. Winbury, Father Murphy and Vera's Rabbi Weiss all thought it was a splendid idea. They were delighted to give us permission to sell cookies and cakes at their places of worship. It was great fun for us and, according to the letters we got back from Minidoka, it did a lot to raise our friends' spirits. "You sent us a gift-wrapped Merry Christmas," Paul Yamaguchi wrote happily. We vowed we'd raise money to send presents every year our friends were there.

I so wished there was more we could do for them, stuck as they were in a camp they couldn't leave, but we sure were thrilled to send them those presents. We were doing *something*.

Vera and Max couldn't wait to see the Nazis get defeated, so all three of us started volunteering to help the war effort any way we could. We rolled bandages at the Red Cross, saved our pennies to buy war bonds, and crocheted scarves in our spare time to send to every one of the people we knew who had joined the service. That included Mr. Winbury's grown-up daughter, Rosette. She had joined the WAACS, the Women's Army Auxiliary Corps, which made her a heroine to every single girl in my class, even Barbara. It also eventually even included Emi's cousin, Nicky Kimura. He was deemed loyal to the USA by however that was determined, not that there was ever any doubt, and had been released from Minidoka to join an all-Japanese Army unit.

Vera and I were asked to sing a few songs as entertainment for the soldiers who came through the hospitality center for service personnel at the train station, another place where we volunteered. Max accompanied us on the piano. It was a lot of fun and we met people from all over the country. All three of us may have been stuck on the home front, too young to join up, but we found all kinds of ways to do our bit to help the war effort.

A letter came from Emi that winter containing some rare good news. "My poor father was finally released from jail, and now he's here with us. He's glad to be with us again but furious that we're all locked up here, including the baby. If I heard this had happened to anyone else I'd think it was absurd. He and my mother both got jobs as cooks for our block's mess hall and they're even enjoying them."

Meanwhile, more people were enlisting in the armed forces. The boys' gym teacher from school joined the Marine Corps. Christopher Callavari's brother Carlo, the one Colonel Barclay had chided back at my dad's going away party for not being in a uniform yet, left college to join the Navy. Mr. Palmer the druggist was too old to go into the service, but he had three sons who all went into the Army together.

Translators who could speak German were also needed for what, rumor had it, was some kind of top-secret war work, and who did they recruit? Vera's father! He went off to New York City to work on a project he wasn't allowed to tell his family one single thing about. It was exciting to wonder about his assignment, but it meant one more dad in our neighborhood was gone.

Mom and I finally found out about the special unit Dad joined. He was training to become a battlefield medic and his job would be taking care of wounded soldiers. He wouldn't be part of the fighting itself. Mom said that was a relief. His odds of surviving were better. "Let's hope we'll keep a *blue* star banner in our window until this war's over, and not have to change it to a gold one," Mom said flatly.

And even my once-timid mother got involved in the war effort. She volunteered to be a local Air Raid Warden. I was so proud of her. She used to say that she didn't have much confidence, but then realized she'd had it all along and let it come forth. No longer a "shrinking violet," Mom patrolled the streets of our neighborhood during blackouts to make sure no lights were visible outside of anyone's houses. I can't honestly say Mom looked snappy in her Air Raid Warden hat – it was like a rounded bowl made of metal, and with a chin-strap, yet – but there she was, doing her bit, banging on the doors of people who let their lights shine through their blackout curtains when they weren't supposed to.

Dad thought it was a spectacular development. "My wife, helping to make Seattle safe from enemy invaders," he wrote. "I'm delighted to hear this! Our city's in good hands now."

Chapter Nineteen – The Other Side of Hoping

Everything and then some began to turn around in the middle of 1944. My father had been posted to the "European theater" of war, as the newspapers called it, just as he'd hoped. He took part in the D-Day Invasion of France on June 6, 1944, the day the Allies landed 156,00 troops there with an armada of five hundred ships to begin freeing Europe from the Nazis' clutches.

"I bet Hitler is having a fit-ler now," Maximillian Manteffel grinned after we heard the announcement.

"It's not that 'the Yanks are coming' anymore, like the song says," Vera smiled. "They've arrived!" That was enough to get us singing "Over There."

By the end of the day, our side was finally winning! The Allies had gained ground in France and were pushing the Nazis back! It was far from over but there was positive progress. Daddy apparently was doing all right in his duties as a medic, or was, at least, as fine as a man can be while treating the wounded on battlefields. It was still dangerous, and it must have been terrifying, but he wasn't in direct combat. We hoped he would come out of the war in one piece. There was still a chance that he wouldn't, which was chilling.

That was the thing about the war: you could go about your business, attend school, act in the class play, roll bandages to help the Red Cross, sing the latest popular songs, ven wind up giving a dancing school a try, once, and yet all the while you could also

ever stop worrying about the people you loved who were in the armed forces. It

nagged at practically everybody on the home front.

Emiko's situation nagged at me, too. I wondered what it was *really* like for her in

Minidoka. She tried to make her letters about the place sound as funny as she could,

but it all seemed like a never-ending nightmare to me. She lived in one drafty wooden

barracks building, went to school in another, ate her meals in a third, washed her

clothes in a fourth, and even had to enter a whole other barracks building, separate

from the one-room apartment where she lived, to shower or go to the bathroom. "From

our room to the Ladies Room is about two Seattle blocks' walk away," she wrote. A

two-block walk in all kinds of weather, just to get to the bathroom! She wrote of

spending a lot of time on lines, especially for meals or showers. "Lines are a great

place to meet new people," she wrote, and cheerfully claimed the whole rotten

experience made her feel "like the pioneers must have felt when they first tried to

conquer the wilderness." Yes, I thought – because the pioneers had an uphill battle on

their hands, too.

Besides, Minidoka might have been presented to the world as a "camp," but those who

were living there were, after all, locked away. They lived behind fences and were

guarded by soldiers in watchtowers. That's soldiers who were armed *with guns*. I knew

that part of the story from Colonel Barclay, and even he had begun to think the idea of

locking every single last one of the West Coast Japanese people away, even the babies,

was going way too far. Well, who wouldn't? Emi made no mention of that part of the

scene at Minidoka in her letters. Good old Emi wrote of pleasant times like winning a camp Jitterbug contest with Paul Yamaguchi to the tune of "In the Mood," singing popular songs in the camp's school choir, and going to the Minidoka Girl Scouts meetings. At harvest time she got out of the camp for a few weeks, long enough to help some local farmers with their beet crop. One day she hid under a blanket in the hay wagon, reading a novel with a flashlight. "It was heaven to be outside of the camp perimeter and just read in peace, quiet – and temporary freedom." She tried to turn whatever happened into funny material, and I thought that was nothing less than heroic under the circumstances.

I wrote back with pleasant stories about singing songs from the new hit Broadway musical *Oklahoma* in seventh grade, and my "As Time Goes By" solo from the wonderful movie *Casablanca* at a concert in the eighth.

I also wrote about our eighth grade play, *Tom Sawyer*, featuring Vera, whose English was finally perfect, as Tom's friend "Becky Thatcher." "I stood up and cheered in the mess hall when I read that Vera, who used to have such trouble with English, was able to play such a big role. Brava!" Emi wrote. "She can't get much more American than to be starring in a Mark Twain story. Did people ever look at me funny in the mess hall when I did that, though, tee hee!"

I wrote about our eighth grade graduation ceremony, when Mr. Winbury misplaced our diplomas and didn't realize it right up until the moment he was there on the stage, about to hand them out. He had to dispatch Miss Bryce to his office to find them and she griped and grumbled the whole way down the auditorium aisle, as only Miss Bryce could do - but she found them. "I can just bet he never forgets those certificates again," Emi eplied. I gave her details about my first week of ninth grade in the high school in

September of 1944, when so many of the other kids felt lost and confused by the big,

new place, but I found I loved being in such a huge school. I told of the silly Senior girls

who fibbed to us "Freshmen" that one of the school staircases was "off-limits to under

classmen," when it wasn't, which made us needlessly avoid it for a whole week. Emi's

eply? "Hilarious, but don't just take that. Think up a good prank to *get them back!*"

I also made certain to tell Emi how, this year in our ninth grade Thanksgiving chorus

show, Vera Manteffel and I, calling ourselves "The Gemstone Girls Minus One," sang a

duet, "Lilli Marlene," that we dedicated to her. It was an oldie but goodie of a number

from World War I, made popular by Emi's good old favorite movie star, Marlene Dietrich.

Before Vera and I began to sing it, I first told the audience about Emi, our missing friend

and fellow Gemstone Girl who was still living in Minidoka camp. I said we hoped she

would be able to come home soon.

Times had changed, thank goodness. Everyone wasn't as terrified of the Japanese-

Americans as they had been, probably because the war was winding down. What I said

actually got a lot of applause, especially from the kids who remembered Emi from

elementary school. Even Emi's father loved the letter I sent about that performance.

He sent a note to say so, along with a little wooden figure he'd carved for me. It was an

angel.

Yet I had to wonder. How in the world were my little stories of school days in Seattle

being received by wrongfully imprisoned people? My biggest problems were easy ones,

like having outgrown my old winter coat and needing to shop for another and couldn't find a color I liked. *They* were living in wooden barracks that weren't even always heated properly. I kept every detail I wrote to Emi and her family as light and pleasant as possible, but still, it seemed almost cruel to tell them about my days running free in the city they had been barred from.

What would any of these people who had been stuck in camps like Minidoka be like when they came back to us? I wondered. What would years of having been prisoners for no reason at all, and living in subhuman conditions, have done to them? Would they be broken by it? I couldn't help but question what they would be like when they were finally allowed home. It had been so long since the happy day when Emi and I had been running through the streets of Seattle singing our "Glow Worm" song and looking forward to that trip to Hollywood we almost went on. That was when we still believed in happy endings like the ones we saw in the movies, and when nobody who knew Emi, at age eleven, would ever have believed she was about to be branded an "enemy" and locked up.

Who would have thought my father would be a battle medic, either? Or that Vera's relatives would be nowhere to be found? Or that millions of people all over the world were in situations that never should have happened, due to a war started by a few very crazy people in positions of power?

And then it was the middle of December of 1944, and one morning I woke up to a surprise. Major-General Henry C. Pratt, Commanding General of the Western Defense Command, issued Public Proclamation 21 about the Japanese people who were still in he camps. The announcement came on December 17, 1944 and it declared that the West Coast Japanese could finally return home as of January 2nd, 1945.

t was the news I never thought would come. January 2nd was just weeks away! I immediately dashed off a letter to Emi, writing, "Hallelujah! You can leave! When will you be coming home?" I hoped she'd be here before she could get a chance to answer.

Everyone was saying it was clear our side would win now, although battles were still raging in Europe, with our soldiers having a tough time that month in Belgium, and in the Pacific, where air strikes were being made on Japanese positions in the Philippines. The fears about "Japanese spies" lurking all over the West Coast had died down. The evacuees could return.

I was home alone after school the next day when Buddy started barking. The doorbell rang a few seconds later. My mother was out shopping.

It was the telegram boy. I was hoping the message would be from Emi's parents, saying "please get our house ready for us, we'll be home soon," so I couldn't help but tear it right open, even though it was addressed to Mom, not me.

It wasn't from Emi's parents.

It was an official notification from some Adjutant-General.

MRS. MARY RAFFERTY =

THE SECRETARY OF WAR DESIRES ME TO EXPRESS HIS DEEP REGRET THAT
YOUR HUSBAND FRANK RAFFERTY HAS BEEN REPORTED MISSING IN ACTION
IN BELGIUM IF FURTHER INFORMATION IS RECEIVED YOU WILL BE PROMPTLY
NOTIFIED

What? I started to sob. Belgium! A major, and very horrific, battle in Belgium had been
all over the news lately. There was a band of lethal Nazis encircling Allied soldiers
somewhere in one of Belgium's forests, in a town called Bastogne, and the conflict there
was raging. Just days before my ninth grade history teacher told our class it was "like
the German answer to Custer's Last Stand. The Nazis simply *will not* give up, but then,
neither will our side, you'll see."

My Daddy, missing in Belgium! With that miserable telegram in hand I now couldn't be
sure of anything. We'd managed to get so far through the war with Daddy being safe,
so how could this be happening now? Yet it was.

I thought of my father on the day, long, long ago, when he had taught me how to ride a
bicycle. Daddy, who made me kites out of tissue paper and taught me to fly them on
the beach by Alki Point Lighthouse, where we'd go on beautiful windy days. My
wonderful father, the proud reporter, who had asked Mom to order a ruby necklace for
me during that first wartime Christmas in case he didn't make it back to give it to me for
my sweet sixteen birthday. He was such a good man. He had been my very own Santa

:laus...and his job in the war was taking care of men wounded on battlefields far from
:ome. What could be better than that?

Vhere was my father? Had the Nazis taken him prisoner? Was he in a prisoner of war
:amp run by those awful Germans? Or was he wounded in some field hospital
,omewhere, maybe too unconscious to tell anybody his name?

Vas he already dead and gone from us forever?

 was almost hysterical by the time Mom showed up. She became upset, too, but kept
assuring me, "The telegram only says he's missing."

 screeched in a manner worthy of Miss Bryce at her most shrill, *"Onlyyyyyyyy?"*

"There's hope for someone who's missing, Ruby! Missing isn't dead."

"He could be!"

"Then we'd be on the receiving end of a telegram worded very differently." Mom tried to
sound optimistic, but there were tears running down her cheeks. "Oh, not now! Not
when the tide is turning so far for the better. Your father can't get killed at this point,
Ruby, when the war's almost at an end."

But it could happen, and both of us knew it.

It was Christmastime again. The one small but nice thing about this particular

Christmas of 1944 was that we didn't have another ultra-small tree. Christopher

Callavari had been at the Christmas tree stand when he ran into my mother and me,

looking for another small tree we could easily get home, when he said he would be

happy to help bring back a large one. When we got it home, naturally Mom asked him

to stay and join us for a mug of hot chocolate, and then an amazing thing happened.

Christopher asked me to go with him to the high school Holiday Dance!

It was the first real date of my life, and my first dance, too. Christopher, bless him,

made it so special. He picked me up on the night of the dance and brought me a white

carnation corsage with a sprig of holly and a red and green ribbon attached. Mom took

pictures with my brownie camera, hoping one day my father would be found and would

get a chance to see what his little girl looked like on this special night.

The high school gym was decorated with lots of red, green and white streamers, a

colorfully lit Christmas tree, and a family of three papier-mache snowmen perched on

white felt "snow" who were positioned up front next to the band. For a few hours we

danced to current hits like "Swinging on a Star, "Don't Fence Me In," and "You Always

Hurt the One You Love," with some Christmas tunes like "Santa Claus is Comin' to

Town" thrown into the mix.

It almost felt like a peacetime Christmas, save for that telegram. Mom and I tried to

enjoy the season but we really just went through the motions. How could we fully have

ourselves a merry holiday when Daddy was on the missing-in-action list? Christmas

Day came, and once again I found myself in our church, praying for the world to

traighten itself out. Would an answer to my prayers ever come? Two new dresses, a
ilver bracelet, and more presents were waiting for me under the tree when we got
ome, and they were wonderful, but all I really wanted for Christmas was some good
ews.

Ve heard nothing further about Daddy that week and started to fear we never would.
Ve didn't hear any news from the Fujiwaras about their plans, either.

Maybe none of them are ever going to return, I started to think. It's entirely possible that
the Fujiwaras would decide not to come back to Seattle but move somewhere else.
Who could blame them, after they'd been forced out of here? And maybe my father
was already...*no!* No, I would not let that thought finish itself, not even inside of my
head.

But who was I kidding? That thought was always there. The chances of our lives ever
returning to anything similar to good old pre-war "normal" seemed to get slimmer during
every day of that long Christmas vacation week. I had several memorable nightmares,
all involving having to replace the blue star banner in our front window with a gold star
one, the one people hung up when they learned their loved one in the service was
never coming back.

Then we heard more details about the "losing" battle in Bastogne, Belgium. The
Germans had the Allies surrounded. It was freezing in Belgium and snowing, too.
Those soldiers who weren't dead from gunshot wounds yet were at risk of dying from

the bitter cold. The German commander actually took pity on our side and tried to offe

our troops a chance of surrendering so that there wouldn't be any more bloodshed.

The message with the offer of surrender was delivered to the American General, MacAuliffe. While he appreciated the offer of putting a stop to the fighting, if he accepted it, that would mean the Allies had given up and the Nazis might win the war. General MacAuliffe wasn't ready to do that. There was never a question of our side giving up.

So General MacAuliffe sent what turned out to be a legendary response to the Nazis:

To the German Commander:

NUTS!

The American Commander

It was said that the German translator had one heck of a time trying to decipher the message.

"That's because 'nuts' doesn't mean 'crazy' in German," Aunt Manya explained with a smile when she heard Vera and me talking about it. "It just means something to eat."

Everything turned around for the better for our side right after that. Reinforcements came through and the Americans continued to win. Even Mom and I began feeling optimistic. The Belgium situation sounded chaotic. Maybe Dad really was alive somewhere in the midst of it.

still had the copy of Mrs. Rivington's poem in my room about hope being "the thing with feathers" that perched in people's hearts and caused their souls to endlessly never stop singing. It caught my eye on December 31st as I was getting ready for the Manteffel's annual New Year's Eve dinner party. I hadn't lost hope about everything one day turning out all right again during all this time, and decided I wouldn't lose heart now, either, but I can't say it was easy.

On the other hand, the Manteffels had an even bigger worry. They still hadn't heard anything at all about the whereabouts of their family members who they hoped had made it to Sweden, but might have gotten stuck in Germany. There was no word whatsoever about their other great-niece, Mitzi, and her mother and father. The Swedish private detective they'd hired to find them hadn't located them yet.

It was known by then that the Nazis' treatment of Jewish people had gotten worse and worse. For years, the Germans had been rounding the Jews up, putting them on trains and shipping them away. No one was entirely sure yet where they were being sent, but given Adolf Hitler's hatred of them, the possibilities were terrifying.

"If they're alive, if they're out there somewhere, we'll find them as soon as the war is over," Uncle Leo said. "I live for the day the rest of my family can be brought here."

"Maybe by this time next year they'll be with us," I said. *Be alive, Mitzi. Be alive, Mitzi's parents. Be alive, Dad.*

Aunt Manya nodded to her husband, "Who knows? It could happen." Yet she no longer sounded like she believed that. Was this war *ever* going to end?

"Where there is life, there is hope," nodded Uncle Leo, but with a rare sigh. It wasn't like him to seem so discouraged. The sight broke my heart.

January 2nd, the first day the Japanese would be allowed to leave the camps, came and went, with still no word from the Fujiwaras. There wasn't any further correspondence from the Adjutant-General of the Army about Dad's whereabouts, either. As for poor Mitzi Manteffel's situation, I had a feeling it was not bound to turn out very well, no matter how much we hoped and prayed to hear otherwise.

School began again and it was a relief to have my classes to concentrate on. The war news kept improving, which was terrific after so many years of setbacks. Surely, people started to say, there would be peace in a matter of months, maybe even weeks. Surely!

On Friday afternoon, January 5, something else happened. The doorbell rang and, once again, it was the telegram boy.

Once again, I was alone in the house after school let out. My mother wasn't there again. One more time, I wasn't going to wait for her to show up before I opened her telegram, either. I signed for it.

Oh please, I thought, ripping the envelope open with hands that were shaking. Oh, my dear loving God, don't let it say that my father's already gone.

But it didn't!

It was good news, *great* news, in fact, the best news possible! It was sent from Daddy himself!

MRS. MARY RAFFERTY AND RUBY RAFFERTY =

ON A HOSPITAL SHIP COMING HOME. MAY HAVE TO STAY IN NEW YORK CITY ARMY HOSPITAL DUE TO LEG INJURIES. OTHER THAN THAT REJOICE ALL IS WELL AND SEE YOU SOON.

FRANK RAFFERTY/DADDY

He was on a hospital ship! He was sailing home to the United States! Okay, I didn't like the part about my poor father having to stay in a hospital in New York with injuries, *but he was alive!* He hadn't been captured, he wasn't a prisoner of war, and even though he was wounded, *he was coming home!*

Mom was delighted when she got home a few minutes later and read the good news, spinning me around and hugging me the way she used to when I was very little. "If that husband of mine does wind up in a New York hospital, do you know what we're going to do, Ruby Carol Rafferty? We're both going on the train to New York the minute we hear about it!"

New York, the home of Broadway! I was about to ask if I could really miss school by going with Mom to that magical city when the doorbell rang again. This time it was Vera along with her Uncle Leo. Both were smiling so brightly they could have lit up the entire west coast during the wartime blackout. "We want you both to come over to the house tonight for a big celebration," Uncle Leo beamed. "We just received great news from our Swedish detective's office. Mitzi and her parents *did* make it to Sweden back in 1939!"

"What!" Mom and I exclaimed in unison.

"It took forever for my contact to find them since they settled temporarily in a very small town and were using a false last name, just in case the Nazis invaded Sweden, too," Uncle Leo relayed. "They were pretending not to be Jewish, just to be on the safe side. They're all right and will be moving to Seattle as soon as the war is over. I can't wait to book them passage on a ship!"

Vera and I danced around the room. I was laughing and crying, both. "She'll be the newest face in our happy crowd," I smiled to Vera.

"I'm going to help her adjust to America, Ruby, the same way you and Emi once helped me," Vera said in her now-perfect English. "Remember how badly I used to speak?"

Hey, you still always managed to make yourself understood," I smiled. "And we just found out good news, too. Great news! My father's on a hospital ship, he's got leg injuries, but he's alive and on the way back from the battlefields!"

Another reason to celebrate tonight," smiled Uncle Leo. For an older man, he looked a lot younger at that happy moment. I guess we all did. Relief could do that to you.

Then above the chatter in the living room I could have sworn I heard someone outside singing. It sounded like that old song Mrs. Rivington had once said was one of her favorites, the one about the bumblebees. I was sure of it.

"Honey keep a-buzzin' please,
"I've got a dozen cousin bees…"

It was a girl's voice.

Could it be?

Was it possible?

We'd had no word…but the voice sounded familiar, just like…

"Who the heck is that out there?" Mom asked. From the bright and hopeful look in her eyes, I think she already knew.

I was just a step away from looking out the window to find out for certain when the doorbell rang yet again. Naturally I ran to get it. Mom was right behind me. And when we opened the door, who did we find on the doorstep?

Mr. and Mrs. Fujiwara with Emi and Hanae! Good old Mr. Winbury was there, too. He had stayed in touch with the Fujiwaras and picked them up at the train station.

"We couldn't wait," Emi told me with a smile. She was a few inches taller. Her hair was cut in a pageboy, and the expression in her eyes seemed a little older and wiser, but she was there, she was back, she was *home*! "We got out of the camp as fast as we could."

"And you're still singing your way up the street!" I laughed. If she could still sing like she always had, I knew that no matter what else had happened to her, some part of her remained all right.

"You better believe it, I am," Emi shot right back with the old mischievous grin I remembered. She put down the suitcase and bags she was carrying.

"The minute I heard that song, I knew it could only be you!" I laughed. Vera and I both rushed over to hug Emi, and then everybody in the room was hugging everyone else.

Mr. Fujiwara had been carrying Hanae, who was no longer an infant. She was almost three and a half years old. He put her down and she scurried over to me.

'm Hanae," she smiled, "and are you Wuby?"

Yes, I am, Hanae, and I've missed you so much!" I knelt down to be closer to her size
nd hug her. "And this lady here is my mother, Mary. This other terrific girl is my friend
Vera, and that's her Uncle Leo."

We got fweedom," Hanae addressed us all in a clear little voice. "We fwee."

You certainly are," I laughed, although I found I was crying some more, too. No more
barbed wire fences or search towers were going to surround this little girl, or the rest of
her family, either. None ever should have in the first place. Well, thank God they were
free!

Emi's mother Noriko smiled, "I guess you can figure out what the baby has been
hearing everybody in Minidoka talking about these last few weeks."

"I'm not the baby now. I'm weally big," insisted Hanae.

"Big enough to go sleigh riding in the snow," I agreed, "so let's hope we get a nice great
big snow storm soon. I'll teach you how to sleigh ride myself. And in the springtime,
Hanae, there'll to be parks for you to visit, and swings for you to ride on, and kites I'm
going to show you how to fly. We'll go to the beach by Alki Point Lighthouse. Right,
Emi and Vera?"

"Right," they chorused.

I was going to make it my mission to find as many ways as possible to make up for all the fun that the little girl had missed when she'd grown up locked behind a fence. My God, she was seven months old when she'd left, so she couldn't have had any memory of anything else!

That's when Emi's dog came dashing into the room, tail wagging. *"Buddy!"* Emi greeted her long-lost pet with open arms. Now she was crying, too. Happy tears. "I sometimes thought I'd never get home to see you again, Buddy."

What a day this was turning out to be! It was hard to believe how fast everything had reversed itself. This was 1945, and I'd started hoping and praying for good news since 1941, but here we finally were. The other side of hoping and praying for good news was actually *getting* it.

One part of me knew, even as I smiled and laughed with the others, that everything was actually far from pre-war perfect. Dad was coming back with an injury. The Fujiwaras had been unfairly locked away, and Mitzi and her parents had been living under false identities. All of them would be coming to Seattle after going through one ordeal after the other. They'd all be changed from the war. But nevertheless they would all *be here!*

"Ruby, I can't ever thank you enough," Mr. Fujiwara said warmly to me. "I understand it was you who came up with the idea for your mother to rent out our house and for Mr. Winbury to find someone to take care of my ice cream shop. Thanks to you, we didn't se them. We're able to come home to both, and most Japanese we know lost everything. You were the answer to my prayers even before I said them."

Me, the answer to his prayers? Wow. I wasn't even sure what to say to that, except the truth, which was, "For all this time I thought I wasn't doing enough to help."

Not true," Emi laughed. "Not true for a big band minute."

We realize there are tenants in our house," Mrs. Fujiwara said to my mother, "but if we could stay here with you for a little while until they can find other arrangements, we would love it."

Otherwise you can always stay with my wife and me," offered Mr. Winbury.

"Or with my family and me," said Uncle Leo.

"You're staying right here with us," said my mother happily. "Ruby and I may be visiting New York if her father is hospitalized there anyway. You could have the place to yourselves and settle back in."

"I would have hung out the biggest welcome home sign you ever saw if only I had known you were coming today, Emi," I grinned. "This is the best day I've had since the day before the war started." I realized she didn't know the rest of the reasons why. "First we got the good news that my father's on his way home on a hospital ship, then a minute before you arrived we heard about a miracle. Vera's cousin Mitzi and her parents are alive, and now here *you* are!"

"You're all invited to a big party at my place tonight," Uncle Leo smiled at the Fujiwara family. "A good-news-all-around party. We'll invite some of your old friends from the school, Emi, and you and your wife, too, of course, Mr. Winbury."

"Would it be possible to include Mrs. Rivington and Miss Bryce?" Emi asked. "I can't wait to see them both. They wrote to me the whole time we were away."

"Of course!" Uncle Leo agreed.

"Maybe Miss Bryce will sing that old favorite song of hers," I grinned, "'A Good Man is Hard to Find.'"

Under his breath, Mr. Winbury muttered, "Uh-oh! Heaven help us."

- The End –

AUTHOR'S NOTE

The internment of "all persons of Japanese ancestry" living on the West Coast of the United States during World War II really happened. It was one of the most shameful chapters in American history. Many Americans, enraged by the unprovoked attack the Japanese Imperial Forces made on Pearl Harbor in Hawaii that killed 2,335 servicemen and wounded 1,143 more, unleashed their fury on the innocent Japanese living among them in the USA. Acts of violence and bullying against those Japanese were common. Fears that these Japanese were "spying" for the Emperor were rampant, as crazy as it sounds in hindsight. This culminated in the forced removal of the Japanese from the West Coast in 1942.

I have attempted, with writing KEEP YOUR SONGS IN YOUR HEART, to be as true as I could to these horrifying events as they took place in Seattle in the 1940's. A wealth of further information on the subject can be found on the website www.densho.org.

Bullying is terrible enough when it's done by children to other children, as happens in this story when Jessup, Chester and Barbara turn on their Japanese schoolmates and their loyal friends like Ruby and Daisy. It's even worse when it's sanctioned and practiced by misguided adults, as happened during the Second World War in quite a few places around the globe. Not only were there actual people like the character of Mrs. Stenzel who gloried in bullying Japanese people living in America, but an entire system of official discrimination also was created against *several* groups of people in

Nazi Germany. That included children just like the characters of Vera and Maximillian Manteffel who had done nothing wrong at all but were misjudged to come from the "wrong" background. One of my own best friends was a Jewish child living under the Nazis and experienced this directly. Yet another wonderful friend wound up living in thi country after her grandparents were discriminated against in the Soviet Union and her parents took her and fled.

There's always some group somewhere who doesn't like another and tries to make it seem "okay" to treat the "others" badly. This was the story of one fabulous little girl named Ruby who knew in her heart that this *wasn't* okay - and didn't turn on her friends. I hope you enjoyed it.

Feel free to reach me through my website, www.carolynquinn.net.

Cheers,

Carolyn Summer Quinn

Made in the USA
Middletown, DE
30 November 2020